MAN.
FOLK
TALES

MANX FOLK TALES

FIONA ANGWIN

ILLUSTRATED BY DENISE McCOID

The
History
Press

First published 2015

The History Press
The Mill, Brimscombe Port
Stroud, Gloucestershire, GL5 2QG
www.thehistorypress.co.uk

Reprinted 2016

Text © Fiona Angwin, 2015
Illustrations © Denise McCoid, 2015

British Library Cataloguing in Publication Data.
A catalogue record for this book is available from the British Library.

ISBN 978 0 7509 6074 8

Typesetting and origination by The History Press
Printed in Great Britain

CONTENTS

ACKNOWLEDGEMENTS

With thanks to all my friends on the Isle of Man, Paul, Mary and Christopher Lewin, John and Sue McKenzie and family, and Linda and Tim Mann, for endless hospitality on my many visits to the Island for performances and research. Also to Richard Angwin and Daniel Jeffrey, for sharing various trips round the Island, and being dragged off to explore obscure sites in my efforts to get to know the place better and research its folk tales for my storytellings and for this book.

Thanks to Daniel Jeffrey for permission to include his version of the Phynodderee story, 'The Phynodderee's Sorrow', and to John Wood, the Managing Director of the Laxey Woollen Mills for permission to include the verse from the mill in 'Manx Tartan'. Thanks are also due to Denise McCoid, my illustrator, for bringing the stories to life so vividly.

Additional thanks to Paul and Christopher Lewin for help with the pronunciation of Manx words. Any mistakes in that respect are definitely mine and not theirs.

Welcome to the Isle of Myth & Magic

Ben-Varrey

fishermen bewitched by these creatures

The Black Dog

Manannan's Home

Tarroo-Ushtey

Witchcraft resides here

Ramsey

Livestock beware

Laxey

Beware the Buggane

St Trinian's

East Baldwin

Peel

The Fairy Bridge

Douglas

Glastin dwell in the sea around here

Dalby

Little People

The Silver Cup

Castle Town

Port Erin

Let sleeping Giants lie

Cregneish

N
W E
S

INTRODUCTION

For anyone who hasn't visited the Island, or noticed its location on a map, the Isle of Man nestles in the heart of the British Isles. It is surrounded not only by water, but also, at a distance, by England, Wales, Ireland and Scotland.

It is, however, a separate country, and the High Court of Tynwald is its Parliament. This is the system of self-government established by its Norse rulers over a thousand years ago, and it still operates today, making it the oldest parliament in the world with an unbroken existence. This means that the Manx people can make their own laws, giving them a sense of freedom and independence.

Tynwald Day is celebrated early in July in the village of St John's. The ceremony takes place on Tynwald Hill, a tiered grassy mound, and it is the Island's annual celebration of its history of self-government. Part of this tradition is that rushes are strewn along the route of the procession to Tynwald Hill as a symbolic tribute to Manannan, the mythical sea god and shape-shifting magician who was the first ruler of the Island. Any new laws that have been passed over the last year are proclaimed in Manx and in English by the Deemsters, the Manx equivalent of British High Court Judges. The Lieutenant Governor of the Island attends the event, along with other dignitaries and civil servants, but it's not all pomp and proclamations, and many of the spectators also go along to enjoy the fun of the fair, which is another traditional element of the celebrations.

As well as having its own laws, the Isle of Man, known as Ellan Vannin in the Manx language, has its own history and culture. In particular it has its own folklore ... and plenty of it!

The Island has a fair-sized human population, and in the past it seems to have had an even larger population of all sorts of other creatures, many of a less conventional kind. It was populated by hideous bugganes, which are fierce and goblin-like and can change their shape and size at will, by the Phynodderee ... a sort of hairy troll-man, and by such a variety of magical and malevolent animals and spirits that it's surprising the Islanders ever dared set foot outside their own front doors.

And then, of course, there are the fairies, not that people ever call them that directly. The Manx people traditionally call them Themselves, the Little Fellows or the Little People (Mooinjer-Veggey in Manx), and these fairies are not tiny glittery creatures with fluttering wings. They are small people, two to three foot tall, who generally wear red caps and green jackets, and are fond of hunting. They are inclined to be mischievous and spiteful ... which is why the Manx are careful to call them such polite names ... you don't want to get on the wrong side of one of these. Even today, when most of the creatures in these stories have been relegated to the past, there is still a strong belief in fairies. Many people call out a greeting to the Little People when they cross the bridge known as the Fairy Bridge, and the trees beside that bridge are usually hung with ribbons, and pieces of paper requesting favours.

The tales I want to tell you in this book will introduce you to all these fantastic creatures and more, and, I hope, to the Island itself, which deserves to be better known than it is.

While I have included a few elements of Manx folklore, most of the book is made up of traditional stories, which have all been written to be read, or told, aloud, and like every storyteller, I've told them in my own way. Some do stick very closely to the traditional tales, others veer away, but in all cases I've listed the sources of the stories at the end of each tale, or, occasionally, acknowledged if the story is completely new. In case you want to tell the tales yourselves,

I've put some phonetic spellings at the end of this book, to help with the pronunciation.

There is an expression used on the Island, which in Manx is 'traa-dy-liooar' (pronounced trair-de-lure). In English it translates as 'time enough', and on the Isle of Man, and in all our busy lives, I hope there will always be time enough for stories.

Fiona Angwin, 2015

1

THE MAKING OF THE MISTY ISLE

THE BATTLE OF THE GIANTS

I *could* tell you how the Isle of Man was made, but you'd call me a liar.
Shall I tell you anyway? I suppose I might as well.
Long ago, when the world was young ...
sometime after the dinosaurs began to disappear, but before the
humans took over the world completely ... *there were giants*!
Great noisy fellows they were, always fighting and shouting,
and this story starts with *two* giants.
(Frankly one giant can cause more than enough trouble on his own,
never mind when two of them get together.)

One of them lived in Ireland, and his name was Finn MacCooil,
and the other was a great red-haired fellow who lived in Scotland,
and these two ... well, they were *always* arguing with each other.
Now you might wonder how two giants living in
different countries could argue much at all, but they managed it.
Finn would stand near the coast of Ireland, and the other giant did
the same in Scotland, so they could see each other in the distance and
hear each other if they shouted loud enough ...
and they could shout very, very loudly!
Some of these quarrels got a little violent,

as giants' arguments often did … sometimes they would stride across
the sea to fight it out in person and on this occasion the Scottish
giant came over to Ireland to have it out with Finn MacCooil.
The battle raged, and they got so angry with each other
that they had a sod fight,
and started throwing great lumps or sods of earth at each other.

The Scottish giant made some particularly rude remark
(which I am not about to repeat when I don't know who
might be listening) and then ran away …
heading out to sea, planning to outrun Finn and make it back
to Scotland. Finn MacCooil, the Irish giant, was enraged by the
insult, as you would have been (think of the worst thing anyone
could say to you, and then imagine it being
ten times worse than that … on second thoughts, don't,
it would be bad for your blood pressure!)
Well, Finn got so angry that he wrenched up an enormous clod of
earth to throw. It was huge, even by giants' standards.

The hole it left in the ground filled up with water and became
Loch Neagh, in Ireland, and even though Finn MacCooil
threw the lump of earth with all his might,
it was so big and so heavy that it never reached Scotland,
but fell into the Irish Sea and became Ellan Vannin,
the Isle of Man.

Once the island was there, of course, people came to live on it …
maybe there were even some people on the massive chunk of land
when Finn grabbed it and threw it into the sea.
He certainly wouldn't have paid any attention to them if
there were, mere humans being rather beneath his notice during a
battle with a fellow giant.

Perhaps because of the unusual way the Island was created,
unusual creatures came to live there,
creatures with a touch of magic about them,

and the most magical of all, of course, was Manannan Mac Y Leirr,
the first ruler of the Isle of Man.

∽

This tale appears in Sophia Morrison's *Manx Fairy Tales* (1911).

LORD MANANNAN, WIZARD OF THE ENCHANTED ISLE

Manannan Mac Y Leirr was the Son of the Sea, and the first Ruler
of Man. He was a great wizard, and so powerful that people later
thought of him as almost like a god. He had a huge stone fortress on Peel Island, and he could use his magic to make even
one single man standing on the battlements look like a hundred
armed soldiers to scare away invaders. When he saw his enemies'
ships approaching, he would cover the Island in a silver mist,
called Manannan's Cloak, to hide it from them. One day, when
he was out walking up on Barrule, he saw that Viking warships
had reached the bay of Peel. Manannan wanted to get down the
mountain quickly, so he turned himself into a shape with no
body and three legs and he rolled down from the mountaintop
like a wheel. When he reached a stream that flowed out into the
harbour he changed back into his human form, then he used the
rushes growing round the water, snapping them into pieces to
make lots of little boats, and floated them down the stream and
out into the harbour. He made them appear to be huge sailing
ships, manned with warriors, and the Vikings, terrified, sailed
away in a panic. So Manannan used magic rather than weapons
to defend the Island, though he had weapons to use if he wanted
them. He had a sword called The Answerer, which would kill
anyone it wounded.

Now the Lord Manannan was the Son of the Sea, and he loved
the water. His ship was called *Wave Sweeper*, and even his horse,
Enbarr of the Flowing Mane, could gallop across the sea as well as
the land. He also had a 'fairy branch' with nine apples of red-gold

upon it. If Manannan shook the branch it played the most beautiful music … so beautiful that it made the listeners forget their sorrows and think only of joyful things.

Manannan was a magician and his wife Faud was an enchantress, and together they lived on the Island and ruled it. They stayed on Peel Island for much of the year, but they had a summer palace up on South Barrule. It was here that Manannan met his people and received his yearly rent from them. Each householder was to bring him one bundle of green rushes, or of hay, every year, depending on what their land produced. They brought these offerings on Midsummer Eve, and as they sat on the slopes of the mountain they would weave mats for his palace by plaiting the rushes. That may be why, to this day, rushes are strewn on the path to Tynwald Hill on Tynwald Day, which is celebrated around midsummer.

They say that a man once tried to cheat Manannan of his yearly gift of a bundle of hay. This man was a lazy, grumpy fellow, who didn't see why Manannan should have the best of his crop, for people always delivered their *finest* sheaf of hay to their ruler. One year, after he had had a bad harvest, mainly because he had been too idle to look after his crops, this fellow took his smallest, mouldiest sheaf of hay up to South Barrule, saying to his wife 'That'll do'. His wife tried to persuade him to take the best of his poor crop instead, but he refused to listen to her. When the man reached the top of the mountain, he threw the mouldy sheaf at Manannan's feet and said, 'Why should I give you *any* of my crop? I'm not your servant!' Manannan stared at the man, amazed, but instead of getting angry at the fellow's rudeness he turned away to talk to some other people who were approaching with their gifts. The moment the man realised that Manannan wasn't looking at him, he snatched the two best bundles of hay he could see, and ran back to his farm with them. He was delighted with himself for tricking Manannan and getting the best of the bargain, and no one any the wiser.

The man gave the stolen hay to his cattle, but they wouldn't touch it, for it seemed that they were more honest than he was.

By the end of the day they were lowing with hunger, and the man went to fetch some of his own hay to feed them, but when he went into his barn, he discovered that *his* hay had blackened and soured ... it was fit for nothing. That was when the man realised that Manannan *had* seen him steal the sheaves, and that the destruction of his own meagre crop was his punishment. Now he would have to sell some of his cows, to have the money to buy fodder for the other animals.

When the man told his wife what had happened she insisted that he went back to see Manannan and say that he was sorry. He argued and grumbled and muttered, for he was terrified to face their ruler, but in the end, he agreed. All that night the man tossed and turned, too afraid to sleep. In those days, if you annoyed a ruler, you could expect to be thrown into prison, at best, or even put to death ... and Manannan was a magician ... surely he could dream up all kinds of other, terrifying punishments? The next day the man climbed nervously up Barrule to apologise to Manannan, who listened to him in silence, and then said, 'You wretched fellow. You're not sorry that you stole from me. You're only sorry that I caught you out. You're too lazy to work hard and grow a good crop of hay, yet quick enough to steal mine when you get the chance.' The man began to shake with fear, expecting the wizard to strike him dead on the spot. The wizard looked at him with compassion, and spoke more gently. 'I will not punish you anymore, this time ... your winter will be hard enough with nothing to feed your cattle, but you must never steal or cheat again. I expect all the people of the Island to be honest from this day.'

Relieved not to be punished any more than he had been, the man worked hard the following summer. The sheaf of hay he brought to Manannan that year was the best on the Island, and the man was *happy* to give it to his ruler. For now he understood that Manannan was a kinder, gentler lord than most, and his people were fortunate to have him to protect them and their Island.

Other versions of the story about the hay can be found, titled 'The Riddle of the Fresh Hay' in *Tales from the Celtic Countries* by Rhiannon Ifans (1999), and 'Grass Rent' in *The Green Glass Bottle – Folk Tales from the Isle of Man* by Zena Carus (1975). Other Manannan stories are to be found throughout Manx folklore and in Sophia Morrison's *Manx Fairy Tales* (1911).

It would seem that Manannan was an exceptionally kind ruler, demanding only a single bundle of hay or rushes a year. The logic of this seems to be that Manx farms were small, and many of the farmers were poor, so the small 'Grass Rent' was a token given to their ruler, rather than a significant share of their crop. It's easy to see the importance of hay, but these days rushes seem less relevant. In the past a heap of rushes in the house could form a comfortable, sweet-smelling bed, or couch. Rushes were likewise strewn across floors to form a sweet-smelling carpet. They could also be woven into mats and turned into rush lights.

The shape that Manannan took to roll down the mountain, 'three legs, without a body, like a wheel', is depicted as the Legs of Man, the symbol of the Isle of Man, and appears around the Island, on the ferries, and on the Lady Isabella, the great waterwheel at Laxey, also known as the Laxey Wheel.

The Manx Cat and Noah's Ark

Noah had built his ark.

The rain was starting to fall … *the flood was coming.*

He had loaded two of every kind of animal on to the ark. Well, he thought he had, perhaps he should double-check. Noah started to count the creatures … two elephants, two tigers, two sheep … he yawned, perhaps he'd better not count the sheep, they were sending him to sleep … but he checked the other animals on his list and they were all there … except one. Noah was worried.

The rain was starting to fall … *the flood was coming.*

One of the cats was missing. The first cat was there, with his nose pressed up against the box with the mice in it, licking his

lips, but where was the second cat? Noah went up on the deck and
looked around … where was that cat?

The rain was starting to fall … *the flood was coming.*

Ah, there she was, chasing a mouse. Looking at the ones on the
ark had made her hungry, but Noah had made it very clear that *no
one* was allowed to eat *anyone* else that was on board, so she had
nipped out to catch one last mouse before they sailed. But …

The rain was starting to fall … *the flood was coming.*

'Cat,' called Noah, 'climb aboard.'

She ignored him … as cats do! She sat there, toying with a mouse,
pausing now and again to lick her paws. Showing off, because, of
course, Noah couldn't possibly leave without her. She was the most
important creature on board.

'Cat, Cat, you've missed your chance,' shouted Noah. 'Who's
out is out and who's in is in!' and he started to close the loading
door of the ark. The cat looked round and saw that they *were* going
to leave without her. She leapt for the door as Noah slammed it
shut … Awwwh! She had made it into the ark, but the door had
closed before she was through it, cutting off her tail. Her beautiful
tail was carried away by the waves. And …

The rain was starting to fall … *the flood was coming … No! …* the flood had *arrived*, and so had the first tailless cat.

The cat was furious, she hated everyone on the ark and sulked for the whole voyage. When the flood was over she made her way to the Isle of Man – which was as far away as she could get from Noah and the others – for she was *still* angry with the lot of them. She had hoped to find her tail on the way, but it was lost forever and ever. Ever since …

The rain started to fall *and the flood came.*

No wonder cats hate the rain!

This story is in *Manx Fairy Tales* by Sophia Morrison (1911) and it is the best-known version of how the Manx cat lost its tail. I've written it down as I tell it, using call and response, but you can just tell it straight, read or spoken aloud. You could add in sound effects like rain sticks, if you have them, it all adds to the feel of the tale. There is an insistent rhythm to this story as the cat runs out of time.

Another myth about the Manx cat is that it's a cross between an ordinary cat and a rabbit … the offspring being the Manx cats, who have relatively small heads, longer hind legs than front legs, a short body and many have a little brush, like a rabbit's, about an inch long, at the base of the lower vertebra as the only sign of a tail. The cat rabbit legend comes from *Tales of the Tailless* by Robert Kelly (2001).

How the Wren became King of the Birds

Long, long, long ago the birds of the air gathered at Tynwald to decide which of them was the cleverest. A lot of squabbling had been going on, and in the end they all agreed that the cleverest bird should be king. The sky was black with birds of all sizes, and every type, come to take their chance to be proclaimed the King of the Birds.

The Corncrake officially announced, 'Ready, Ready'. Then each of the birds got up in turn to tell of all the great things they could do. The Falcon boasted that he and his mate were worth the Kingdom of Mann. The Thrush sang to them, and it was a pleasure to listen to her. The Goldfinch spread her bright plumage, and the Swallow told of her swiftness and travels to warm countries in the south.

The Curlew stepped forward to tell them of her riches, 'Let the curlew be poor or fat, she carries a groat upon her back,' said the bird, showing the coin-shaped mark she bears.

When the Cuckoo got up, the Meadow Pipit darted forward and danced round saying, 'Let every bird hatch her own eggs,' so poor Cuckoo wasn't heard at all.

The Magpie and the Jackdaw started arguing loudly about which was the best thief.

At last little Jenny Wren got up to have her say, after all the grand ones had had their turn. The other birds laughed at her, but Jenny Wren got the better of them for all that, saying, 'Small though I am and slender my leg, twelve chicks I can bring out of the egg.'

And the birds agreed that Jenny was as clever as the best of them, and deserved to be their leader, but the eagle didn't like the idea of a little bird like Jenny Wren being more important than him. So he called out, 'Birds, it's only right that the best bird on the wing should be king. Let's see which of us can go the highest before we decide.' Most of the birds thought that this would be fair, so the Cormorant gave the whistle to fly and instantly off they started. Spreading his great strong wings, the eagle led the way, the smaller birds following behind him. But the Bat, the Stonechat, the Cuckoo and a few others, they didn't stir. The sleep had fallen on them and they missed out on the contest.

The Eagle flew up higher and higher, until he couldn't rise up any more. Then he peered down towards the birds far, far below, and screamed, 'I am the King of the Birds!'

But little Jenny Wren was too clever for him; she had taken tight hold of the eagle by a feather on his back, and been carried up into the sky with him. When he screamed, 'I am the King of the Birds!' she flew up on top of his head and called out, 'Not true, not true … I'm above him.'

Down dropped the Eagle, defeated and angry, and down dropped the Wren, the King of the Birds … or, in this case, the Queen.

From *Manx Fairy Tales* by Sophia Morrison (1911).

I'm not quite sure why the bat is in this story, along with the birds, but often in folklore the place of the bat is considered ambiguous … sometimes classed as an animal, sometimes as a bird.

THE CORMORANT AND THE BAT

Now friendship is a wonderful thing, and those who find a true friend are very fortunate. The creatures in this story were just such friends, who had sworn to support each other through thick and thin. The two creatures were a cormorant and a bat, and they were devoted to each other.

Long ago when the Island was young, life was difficult. The people were struggling, and these two kindly animals wanted to do something to help, so they decided to travel around the Island, gathering scraps and twists of wool to make into clothing for the poor. When they had gathered a decent amount, they decided it was time to take it to an old lady that the cormorant knew of, to ask her to turn it into clothing. They were loading the wool into a boat, pulled up on the shore, for they had agreed that the best way to get the fleece to this lady was by boat. As they got ready to put to sea, they didn't notice that a seagull was listening to their conversation.

Now this seagull had been watching these two animals and observing their friendship, and he was jealous. Although he tended to travel with others of his own species, he didn't have any friends of his own, as he wasn't a kind or friendly creature. He overheard the bat and the cormorant agreeing that whatever happened, they would stick together until the job was done, and the wool was delivered. The seagull didn't believe that any creature would put itself at risk for another, since he wouldn't do so himself, and he flew away, unimpressed.

Once the pair had put to sea, a storm came on, so fierce that the waves were breaking over the vessel so that the poor bat, who was only small, had to leap from place to place to escape the water, and in the darkness he was washed out of the boat, only staying afloat by clinging to an oar. At daybreak he was near the shore and flew on to dry land. He was desperately concerned for the cormorant's safety, and resolved to go and search for his friend as soon as he got his strength back.

Along came the very same seagull, who asked the bat what had happened, and on hearing the bat's story, the seagull said, 'I wouldn't go looking for your friend, if I were you. You promised to stay with him until you completed your task. You broke your promise, and if he sees you, he'll kill you.' The bat protested that his friend the cormorant would never be so cruel. After all, he hadn't left the boat by choice. The seagull, however, being jealous of their friendship, didn't see why they should have the pleasure of each other's company when he himself was always alone. He nagged and nagged away at the bat, insisting that the cormorant would be after his blood because of the broken promise, and eventually the seagull had the poor little creature confused and convinced.

The bat was so frightened that he hid himself in an old ruin until the night came, and from that time on he only came out under the cover of darkness. Although he got on with his life in the dark, he mourned for the loss of his dear friend, and not a day went past without him wishing that the wave hadn't washed him out of the boat, making him break his promise.

The cormorant, who was also battered by the storm, had clung to the boat until she filled with water and sank to the bottom of the sea. At last the bird flew to a rock, and there sat for hour after hour, day after day, looking out for the bat. It never for a moment occurred to the cormorant that his best friend was now afraid of him, for he had understood completely that the bat had been carried away by the waves, and had never intended to break his promise. Sometimes the cormorant would go to the glens for a season, searching for his missing friend, and other times he carried on looking sadly out to sea.

If it wasn't for the interference of the jealous seagull, the friends might have been happily reunited. Instead, from the night of the storm until today, one hides himself away, while the other searches for him ... and both of them grieve for the loss of their friendship.

From *Manx Fairy Tales* by Sophia Morrison (1911).

THE ENCHANTRESS

These days you can't open a magazine or turn on the television without seeing people who are beautiful ... and not just beautiful but stunning, so much so that often we take it for granted. Of course, sometimes their looks are enhanced by make-up, lighting, fancy diets or even surgery. In the past, people didn't have all those options. You might think that a person could only be beautiful back then if their beauty was natural, and that was true, of course, for most people. Yet every rule has its exception, and the exception in this case was witches. No, seriously, I know what you're thinking ... most peoples' idea of a witch is an ugly old crone, with a humped back, hooked nose and a broken-toothed grin.

Well, perhaps some of them did look ugly, but you have to remember that this is a bit of a caricature, and while most of them were simple wise women, others had magic ... and with magic came choices. One of these witches made a *choice* to look beautiful. Terribly beautiful!

Her name was Tehi-Tegi, and she was a powerful enchantress. Now she didn't just make herself pretty in a 'she looks nice' kind of way ... she didn't even go for beautiful in a 'fit to be a Queen' way. Oh no ... she went for 'so utterly, devastatingly gorgeous that every man who looked at her fell in love with her on the spot'.

And it wasn't just the humans who came under her spell. When she went out for a walk the birds themselves forgot to sing because they were so busy staring at her, and her sweet voice would tempt them down from the trees to listen. As for the other animals, her beauty entranced them too. They came out of their burrows, or crowded to the edges of their fields to look longingly at her, hoping for even a moment of her attention. Only the cats turned away, casually, as if they didn't care. Of course they *did,* but they were too proud to show it.

Men travelled from all over the Island to be with her, and once they saw her face, they never wanted to leave ... her enchantment drove everything else out of their heads. They forgot all about their wives and sweethearts, they forgot to tend their fields and their livestock. They forgot everything else in the world, all their joys and sorrows, hopes and fears, until, at last, the life of the Island ground to a halt, because the men were so taken up with following this enchantress that nothing else was getting done at all. No crops were planted or harvested, and the seasons came and went, unnoticed. The men followed Tehi-Tegi wherever she led, hoping to be the one to catch her eye and win her hand.

Perhaps this was understandable amongst the handsome young men, but *all* the men on the Island were following her round ... old men, boys, those who had no hope of attracting her attention, they all trailed after her, enraptured by her appearance. Many of these men were already married but Tehi-Tegi's beauty made them forget the very existence of their wives, and whenever one of them could get her alone they would propose to her. Instead of just saying 'No', for in truth she wasn't interested in any of them, she always said 'Maybe I will', leaving each man thinking that *he* was the one she favoured, the person that she would marry one day.

Of course, the women of the Island didn't just sit around doing nothing. They worked the land, and tried to keep things going, but without any men to help them, things were increasingly difficult. They went after their husbands and sweethearts too, trying to convince them to return to the lives that they had left behind. Some of the wives even dragged their children after them, in the hope that seeing their sweet innocent faces would break the hold the enchantress had over their husbands. The men, however, looked straight through their former loves, as if they were no more than memories.

When she had most of the men on the Island under her spell, Tehi-Tegi announced that she wished to ride across the Island, and that the men could follow her on foot, if they chose. There was a flurry of activity, as the men vied with each other to fetch her milk-white horse, which they had been taking it in turns to care for. It was the only creature they'd paid any attention to for months, and it was beautiful … almost as lovely as the woman who rode it.

From a distance it would have looked like a jolly procession, with the enchantress in the lead. She wore her best white gown, and had flowers woven into her hair … though all the men agreed that Tehi-Tegi needed no adornment. Her horse, too, was a fine animal, with a jewelled harness and neat little hooves shod in gold, clip-clopping along in front. The enchantress had a look of triumph on her face as she led her followers through the countryside.

She rode to the bank of a glittering, fast-flowing river. She could see at a glance that it was dangerously deep, but she used her magic to make it seem shallow … little more than a gentle stream that even a child could wade through. The smile on her face twisted into a gloating expression as she began to ride across the river, picking her way slowly towards the far bank so that all the men could follow her at their own pace.

Once her victims were in the river, however, she broke the spell that had made it look safe and raised a great wind, which lashed the water this way and that, until every man was overwhelmed and drowned. Six hundred men were lost that day, and only a handful, those who were still on the bank, waiting their turn to enter the water or just starting to cross, were left alive.

Now one of these men had a wife who was determined to get her husband back, for she loved him dearly, and she didn't trust the enchantress at all. She had been keeping an eye on her man from a distance for weeks, and had followed the procession on foot herself, keeping well back so that Tehi-Tegi didn't spot her. As her love began to step into the water, she grew suspicious and ran forward to grab hold of his arm, dragging him back. At first he tried to twist away from her, but as the spell broke and the others drowned before his eyes, he ceased his struggles and watched the disaster unfold in horror. Those were the two who saw what happened next, for the other survivors were too busy pulling themselves out of the raging torrent. What happened next was this ...

Both the horse and rider were in the water themselves, and it looked as if these two would also drown, but before the eyes of the couple on the bank, the enchantress turned her milk-white mare into a porpoise, which plunged to the bottom of the river and made its way out to sea. Tehi-Tegi transformed herself into a bat and took to the air, spinning and wheeling in delight at the success of her trap, then flew off into the distance and was never seen again. As soon as she was out of sight her hold on the rest of the survivors was lost. They crawled out of the water, gazing at each other in horror, suddenly remembering all that they had left behind, and terrified at how close they had come to death. When they got home they had a lot of making up to do with their wives and families and sweethearts ... though most of the women were just thankful that their men were among those few who had escaped alive, and didn't give them too hard a time. After all, there were six hundred families grieving for the death of their loved ones, and for them, life would never be the same again.

However, it was agreed afterwards that something had to change, so that such a disaster could never happen again. The solution, or so it was thought at the time, was that the women should go on foot from then on, and follow *behind* their husbands wherever they should lead, but never to step out in front.

This custom was stuck to so rigidly for a while, that if by chance a woman was seen walking ahead of a man, whoever saw her would cry out 'Tehi-Tegi!' as a reminder of the dangerous enchantress.

Tehi-Tegi is a name, and not a Manx word, so I can't give you any pronunciation clues for this one ... just take a stab at it!

This story can be found in *The Folklore of the Isle of Man* by A.W. Moore (1891) and *Manx Fairy Tales* by Sophia Morrison (1911).

Some versions of the tale say that she turned into a wren, rather than a bat.

2

THE COMING
OF THE VIKINGS

THE LEGEND OF THE LOGHTAN

Long ago, on the Isle of Man, all the sheep looked just like sheep do
everywhere, white and fluffy, and only the rams, the males that
is, had horns. Then the Vikings arrived! Everyone was terrified,
including the sheep. When the Vikings first landed,
they weren't interested in farming, or being shepherds.
They just wanted to steal what they could carry off,
and destroy everything else …
That's how it seemed to the sheep, anyway.

So the Great Ram who led the flock went to see the Wizard,
Lord Manannan, up on the mountain and asked for help to
protect his people, the sheep. Manannan, the Great Wizard,
peered down at the ram and said, 'Very well, Little Ram,'
for the creature didn't seem like a Great Ram to him, 'You may
have three wishes, but you must use them to protect your flock.'

Now the Great Ram wasn't particularly clever,
in fact the only good idea he'd ever had was to go and see
Manannan, so he wasn't sure what to wish for.
Manannan looked down patiently and asked,

'Well, what's your first wish?'
'Der … I don't know,' said the Great Ram. 'What do you think?'
'Well, tell me,' said Manannan kindly,
'who are the weakest in your flock?'

'Der … that would be the little white lambs,' answered the ram.
'They are easy to see on the hillsides so they are
the most obvious targets … too weak to protect themselves,
or to run away from the invaders. They can bounce about,
but that's not the same as escaping.
Maybe you could make them harder to see?'

'Very well, Little Ram,' said the wizard, smiling,
'from now on the lambs shall be black in colour when they are born,
and for the first few weeks of their lives,
so that it will be harder for the Vikings to see them. What else?'
'Der ... I don't know,' said the Great Ram, again.
'What do you think?'

Manannan could see that this might take a while,
so he gave the ram a clue:
'Well, if changing the colour of the *lambs* was a good idea?'

'Yes, I know, I know!' said the ram, excitedly.
'You could change the colour of the *adults* too. Make them ...
not white, which is so easy to spot on the hillside
that the Vikings can find us easily.'

'Very well, Little Ram,' said Manannan.
'What colour would you like your flock to be?'
'Der ... I don't know,' replied the ram.
'Make them the colour of something that
is good at hiding, like a mouse. Make us ... brown.'

'Very well, Little Ram,' said the wizard wearily.
'From now on your flock shall be mouse brown,
which is lugh dhoan in Manx,
so you shall be known as Loghtan sheep.
You still have one wish left, Little Ram, what's it to be?'

'Der ... I don't know,' said the ram, giving his usual answer.
'My brain aches from all this thinking, I've run out of ideas.'

'Come on Little Ram,' said Manannan, starting to get impatient,
'use your head!'

'My head ... of course!' answered the ram, 'I have a wonderful pair
of horns on my head. But *more* horns would be better ...

give me two pairs of horns ... or even three pairs.
Then I would have *six* wonderful, curly, great long horns that
I can use to defend my flock ... but there is only one of me.
What if *all* my flock had horns, the females as well, to defend
themselves with when hiding isn't enough? That would be perfect!
Please, give them all horns ... but make the females' horns a bit
smaller than mine and the other males, so that the females don't
start thinking that they're in charge.
I don't want them bossing me about.'

'Very well, Little Ram,' said Manannan, thankful the meeting was over,
'if it's horns you want, horns you shall have!'

Mannanon did as the Great Ram asked and to this day Loghtan
sheep are born black, turn mouse brown when they are older,
and *all* of them, males and females, have horns ... one or two,
or even three pairs of horns each.

And so they survived the invasion of the Vikings, and all the other
changes on the Island ... and the Loghtan sheep can still be found
on the Isle of Man to this day!

❧

This is a new story so I can't put lots of references in. There are lots
of stories to explain why Manx cats are so unusual, but nothing
about the remarkable Loghtan sheep. I decided they deserved a
story too, so here it is, and I hope you enjoyed it!

MANX CATS AND VIKING HELMETS

Once all the cats on the Isle of Man had beautiful, long, elegant
tails, but when the Vikings came, things changed. Vikings were
fierce, Vikings were mean, Vikings were scary ... but they were
really into fashion. They liked to carry fancy axes, they liked to

❧

wear fine embroidered tunics and they especially liked to decorate their helmets with tails, and the best tails to use were, of course, cats' tails! So when the Vikings arrived on the Isle of Man, they kept their eyes peeled for cats. If they saw a cat wandering across the path, they would run after it, and use their axe to chop the cat's tail off, and then fix it on to their helmet. And the Vikings didn't want just one tail each, oh no, every Viking wanted as many tails as possible ... they were the latest 'must have' fashion accessory!

In their eagerness to get the tails, the Vikings weren't always very humane, or careful. They didn't take the cats to a vet, or use an anaesthetic, they'd just slash around with an axe and sometimes they'd cut off the tail ... but sometimes they were clumsy and they cut off the head instead.

Now the mother cats weren't too keen on the Vikings coming along and killing their babies, so they started to chew off their kittens' tails as soon as the babies were born, so that the Vikings would leave their little ones alone. They did this for generation after generation, until eventually Manx cats came to be born without any tails at all.

Times have changed and Vikings, and their helmets, are no longer in fashion (with or without the cats tails) but Manx cats will always be fashionable, because they're so unusual ... precisely because they *don't* have beautiful, long, elegant tails.

This is one of a number of stories on the Island about why Manx cats don't have tails. Obviously, in terms of genetics, this is not a realistic explanation ... but it does make a cracking story, doesn't it?

From *Tales of the Tailless* by Robert Kelly (2001).

3

THE ARRIVAL OF THE CHURCH

THE FATE OF MANANNAN

Ellan Vannin, which is the Manx name for the Isle of Man, was ruled over by the wizard, Manannan, for many long years, but not anymore. When St Patrick came to the Isle of Man, he banished Manannan and all of his followers, and they left the Island, but Manannan couldn't bear to go too far from his beloved home.

He and his friends left the Island in their three-legged form, without human bodies. They rolled across the land like wheels, travelling over the water too, and came to a smaller island. Some people say it's south-west of the Calf of Man, others are sure it's near Port Soderick on the south-east coast, but all agree that Manannan used his magic to drop this little island to the bottom of the sea, and there he and his followers made their home, hidden from sight.

Once every seven years, however, it rises up from the sea just before sunrise, and Manannan gets to look once more at his beloved Ellan Vannin, the Isle of Man. The hills of his small, enchanted isle are green, and white foam laps at the edges of the land. If you could get near enough you might see the golden hair of the mermaids, the ben-varrey, as they sit beside the water's edge, washing their jewels. The birds sing loudly on the island then as if it was the first morning of the world, and the scent of the flowers growing there is carried over the water on the breeze. However, this beauty is short-lived, for after thirty minutes, as the first rays of the sun touch the tops of its highest hills, the island sinks back into the sea.

If, during the brief time when the island is visible, anyone is brave enough to get across to it by boat and place a Bible on any part of the land, and so sanctify it, the enchantment might be broken and it would remain above the waves forever. However, if the attempt fails, sadly the enchantment turns against the one who tried to take the blessing to the island, and that person quickly sickens and dies.

Now on one occasion a long time ago, at about the end of September on a fine moonlit night, Nora Cain was strolling along the little bay in Port Soderick, arm in arm with her young man. They had stayed out much later than intended, planning their wedding and talking about the future, and morning wasn't far off. Nora noticed something in the distance, out to sea, which seemed to be growing in size as she watched. Now many a time and oft the girl had heard her old grandfather tell the tale of the enchanted island at Port Soderick as they sat beside the turf fire on a winter's evening. The idea struck her that this distant shape must be none other than the enchanted isle itself.

Suddenly Nora let go of her young man's arm and hurried home as quickly as she could. She ran into the house calling out, 'The Bible, the Bible, the Bible!' After hastily explaining what she had seen, she grabbed the precious book and ran back to the beach, but she didn't even have the time to jump into a boat and begin to row towards the island. Indeed, she was only just in time to see the top of the enchanted isle sink once more under the waves for another seven years.

From that night poor Nora gradually sickened and pined away, and was soon followed to her grave by her young man, who died, it was thought, of a broken heart. It is said that from that time no one has been brave enough to make the same attempt, in case they fail and the enchanter has his revenge on them, or even punishes the whole of the Isle of Man, for disturbing his refuge.

The first section of the 'Traditionary Ballad' in *The Folklore of The Isle of Man* by A.W. Moore (1891) gives the following account of St Patrick banishing Manannan:

> Then came Patrick into the midst of them;
> He was a saint, and full of virtue;
> He banished Manannan on the wave,
> And his evil servants all dispersed.
> And of all those that were evil,
> He showed no favour nor kindness,
> That were of the seed of the conjurors,
> But what he destroyed or put to death.
> He blessed the country from end to end,
> And never left a beggar in it;
> And also cleared off all those
> That refused or denied to become Christians.
> Thus it was that Christianity first came to Man,
> By St Patrick planted in,
> And to establish Christ in us,

And also in our children.
He then blessed Saint German,
And left him a bishop in it,
To strengthen the faith more and more,
And faithfully built chapels in it.
For each four quarterlands he made a chapel
For people of them to meet in prayer;
He also built German Church in Peel Castle,
Which remaineth there until this day.

The story of the submerged island appears in A.W. Moore's book too, as well as in *Manx Fairy Tales* by Sophia Morrison (1911) and *The Folklore of the Isle of Man* by Margaret Killip (1975).

IVAR AND MATILDA

'Childhood sweethearts', that's the phrase we use for two young people who have grown up together, gradually moving from friendship to love. And 'childhood sweethearts' was what Ivar and Matilda were. It was a long time ago – 1249 to be precise – but some things don't change … and love is love, whatever the century.

Now at the time of our tale, Ivar had grown into a gallant young knight and Matilda was a beautiful young woman. Perhaps if she had been less beautiful, things would have gone more smoothly for them both … and Ivar would have loved her just as much, for he knew what she was like on the inside, and cherished her for that too, as much as he did his own soul.

At this period Reginald was King of the Isle of Man and, according to ancient custom, Ivar had to present his betrothed at the Court of the Monarch and obtain the king's consent to their marriage. The wedding day had already been fixed, the feast had been prepared, and all the important people on the Island had been invited. King Reginald resided in Rushen Castle, and that's where Ivar had to take his bride-to-be. Dismounting from their horses at the entrance to the keep, they were conducted to the king's chambers. Ivar doffed his jewelled cap and bowed, then, leading forward Matilda, he presented her to the king.

Matilda, however, was so beautiful that King Reginald wanted her for himself. I will not say that he fell in love with her, for love would have taken account of her feelings, and he did not. He wanted to own her, possess her, and claim her for himself. To achieve this, he made false accusations against Ivar and banished him from his royal presence, detaining the beautiful maiden.

Matilda was devastated by the king's actions. Although Reginald tried to calm her down, she refused to listen to his talk of devoted love, for she saw his compliments for the hollow words they were. Exasperated at her resistance, he had her imprisoned in one of the most isolated rooms in the castle. Reginald expected that after a few days the girl would accept him and see the advantages in being partnered with a king rather than a mere knight. Which just goes to show that Reginald didn't understand love at all. He didn't understand the duties of being a king either. He had only been the monarch for less than a month, and all he could see was the power of the position, not its responsibilities.

Ivar, of course, tried to clear his name and denounce the king, but everyone was too afraid of Reginald's power over them, so no one dared support the young knight. Left without his love and his position, he decided to join the monks at the monastery of St Mary's in Rushen, who welcomed him with joy, and sympathised with him for all that he had lost. Ivar was determined to devote himself to doing good works and helping others, since he could not help himself, but he couldn't get Matilda out of his thoughts … he didn't even know if she was alive or dead. One day, Ivar, having completed his duties, was wandering through the woods, thinking of his betrothed, when he noticed a narrow crevice in a large rock off to the side of the path. Being curious, he approached it and discovered that it was the entrance to an underground passage. After lighting a stub of candle that he carried in his pouch, he squeezed inside and found that he could walk upright in the tunnel. Travelling for some distance, he came to a door, which he forced open.

Suddenly a piercing shriek, which echoed through the passages, made him freeze, horror-struck, for a moment. It was repeated faintly several times. He hurried onward, following the sound, until he saw a faint glimmer of light ahead and found himself in a vaulted chamber. Passing through it, another cry met his ear. Rushing impetuously forward, he heard a voice in a state of exhaustion call out, 'Mother of God, save Matilda!' Through a crack in the next door, he saw his love, Matilda, pale and dishevelled, struggling in the arms of King Reginald, who had finally run out of patience with her constant refusals. Ivar instantly burst through the door, seized the king's sword, which had been left carelessly on the table, and plunged it into Reginald's heart.

The young knight, carrying Matilda in his arms, continued on through the subterranean passage, which brought them to the sea where they hired a boat, to carry them to Ireland. Killing the king, however justifiably, meant that they could no longer remain on the Isle of Man. Once in Ireland they were married at last, and passed the remainder of their days in loving partnership, strengthened by mutual admiration and gratitude … childhood sweethearts united at last.

෨

This romantic tale can be found in *The Folklore of the Isle of Man* by A.W. Moore (1891). Moore quotes the *Chronicon Manniae* account that, 'In the year 1249 Reginald began to reign on the 6th May, and on the 30th May of the same month was slain by the Knight Ivar and his accomplices.' The *Chronicon Manniae* (which translates as *A Chronicle of the Kings of Man*) was supposedly written by the monks of Rushden Abbey and at least one of the entries dates back to 1313, making this the oldest story in the book, but by their very nature folk tales are hard to pin down.

The disparity in these two dates is due to the story being written down sixty-four years after the events took place. This also means that it would have been handed down by word of mouth, and probably embellished, before it was put down on paper, or in this case, vellum. All writers and storytellers embellish their tales, as you've probably already realised.

The description that A.W. Moore used in his version of the story was a bit too much like a bodice-ripper for me. Ivar '… beheld his long lost love, with dishevelled hair and throbbing bosom, in the arms of the tyrant Reginald …' Quite racy for 1891! Times and tastes do change, even though stories last forever … and nobody tells a story without altering it a little.

ST MAUGHOLD AND THE BELLY OF THE FISH

Over in Ireland long ago, there was a band of murdering robbers, led by a chief called Macaldus. He was angry with St Patrick, because many of his robbers had listened to the saint, laid down their weapons and turned to God. Which meant, of course, that they didn't want to work for Macaldus anymore. So when the robber chief heard that St Patrick would be passing nearby on a certain day, the remaining band of robbers lay in wait, intending to kill the saint. When they saw St Patrick though, they found that they couldn't bring themselves to attack him. Determined to make fun of him instead, Macaldus had one of his men lie on the ground and pretend to be dead, and then they called out to St Patrick, asking him to come and pray for the dead man. Realising that it was a trick, the saint refused, and walked on, so Macaldus told the man to stand up. That was when they discovered that the man really was dead, even though he had been healthy enough only a few minutes before. They ran after St Patrick, apologised for the trick and told him what had happened, and he willingly came back to pray for the man, now that his need was real.

The saint prayed over the dead man until life and breath returned to him. All of the robbers decided to accept the Christian faith that St Patrick preached, and Macaldus, who had been the worst of them, asked the saint to set him some penance or punishment, so that he could endure it willingly, to show that he was sorry for all that he had done wrong. St Patrick told him that no penance was needed. If Macaldus had faith in Christ then he was forgiven of *all* he had done wrong in the past already.

However, Macaldus insisted on being set some punishment, so St Patrick led the robber chief to a small boat on the River Boyne. The saint took a boat chain and wound it around Macaldus. He fixed the chain in place with a padlock, snapped the lock shut and threw the key into the river. Then he told Macauldus to get into the boat and said, 'Don't release the chains that bind you until that key is found and brought to you. Be truly sorry for your past mistakes, and learn to pray. Trust to God to show you where to go, and He will lead you.' Then the saint cast off the little boat and Macaldus drifted away down the river and on to the sea.

The next day the dejected figure of Macaldus, in his little boat, was carried by the tide into a harbour on the Isle of Man. Some fishermen helped him ashore and took him to see the bishop, who lived nearby. Macaldus explained what had happened and asked the bishop to teach him more about the Christian faith. The kind old man taught him willingly, and Macaldus studied hard, despite the difficulty of working in chains, but whenever people offered to break the chains, or saw them through to set him free, he refused. After years of study, Macaldus was about to be ordained as a priest himself, and the bishop threw a great

feast to celebrate. The cook had bought a huge fish at the market and was gutting it, and preparing it for the meal, when he found something inside its stomach. He ran to the room where the bishop and Macaldus were studying and cried, 'Look what I've just found in the belly of a fish.'

It was the key to the padlock, the very key that St Patrick himself had thrown into the river all those years before. The bishop unlocked the padlock, and Macaldus was ordained priest the next day without any chains, happy that he had served his penance willingly, and proved that he was sorry for all he had done wrong in the past … and when the kind old bishop died, many years later, Macaldus went on to become Bishop of Man, and came to be known as St Maughold.

This story appears in A.W. Moore's *The Folklore of the Isle of Man* (1891).

4

THE IMPORTANCE OF THE LITTLE PEOPLE

THE TIME THIEF

Long ago, when the Island was a green and pleasant place, the fairies moved around freely, but with the coming of the railway and the increase in the human population, the Little People were driven into the last few quiet places, like the orchards of country cottages.

There was once a poor Manxman who wanted to marry a girl from a wealthy family. The two young people were deeply in love, but the girl's parents refused to let them marry, because the young man had no money of his own. One night, as the young man was wandering through his orchard, he saw a fairy burying her gold under one of his apple trees. He hid until she was gone, and then the young man dug up the fairy's gold, seven bags of it in all. He took this gold to the father of the girl he wanted to marry. The old man couldn't believe his eyes when bag after bag of gold was emptied on to the table in front of him. Well, now that the young man was rich the father was happy to give his permission for the couple to marry, and the wedding was arranged.

They made a fine day of it, with everyone in their best clothes, and food and drink for all who came to celebrate. The young man thought his bride had never looked lovelier than she did that day, standing in the church in her wedding gown, with flowers in her hair and a loving smile on her face.

On the evening of the wedding, when everyone else was still busy celebrating, the young man crept away from the party and went quietly out to the orchard, hoping to find more money, though in truth he already had more than enough for his needs. Instead he found the fairy he had stolen from, sitting under one of the fruit trees, weeping because of her missing gold. Feeling guilty, the young man explained that he had needed the gold so that he could marry his love. They talked together in the moonlight for what seemed like a few minutes, and then the fairy told him to return to his bride. He thought the fairy had kindly forgiven him, but he was wrong.

He walked back to his cottage, but as he approached it, he found that the wedding guests had gone, and the house was quiet. When he entered, he saw that there was a man he didn't know sitting in a chair by the fire. His lovely bride was no longer in her wedding dress, but had already changed into her normal clothes. She was busy getting two little children ready for bed. The young man stared at the children, wondering whose they were. Had his bride been asked to look after some young relatives, on her wedding night? When the woman looked up and saw him, she turned pale, and cried out, 'Where have you been? Why did you leave? What did I do to upset you?'

He didn't understand what she meant, for surely he'd only been gone a few minutes. The strange man stood up and put his arm protectively around the woman's shoulders, as she went on to explain, 'You walked out on our wedding night, seven years ago, and never came back, or sent me word of why you'd gone or where you were.' It seemed that she had waited for him for three years, and then abandoned all hope of him returning. She had married another man, the one who stood beside her now, and he was the father of her two little children.

The young man, heartbroken, turned and left the cottage, and was never seen again. It seemed that the fairy hadn't forgiven him after all. He had stolen the fairy's seven bags of gold, and she had stolen seven years of his life in revenge.

❧

This story appears in *Fables, Fantasies and Folklore of the Isle of Man* by Harry Penrice (1996).

THE FIDDLER AND THE FAIRY FOLK

There was once a young man who was the best fiddler on the whole Island. That was how he made his living, wandering around the Island playing at weddings and funerals and parties, earning a penny here and a penny there. He could earn enough to live on that way ... but the young man wanted to get married, and how could he afford to buy his own cottage and a little piece of land just by earning a few pennies playing the fiddle? There was a young lady he'd set his heart on, but would she be willing to wait until he could afford to take a wife?

❧

Well, one night he was walking home, having played his fiddle at a wedding near Ballasalla. The shortest route to his home in Bradda was over the Fairy Hill, and being worn out and ready for his bed, the fiddler walked that way. At the top of the Fairy Hill was a circle of tall standing stones, and as he reached them he noticed one of the Little People, sitting on a rock and playing a small flute. The little man's music was so beautiful that the fiddler stopped to listen, and he soon found himself joining in on his own instrument. They played together for an hour or so ... jigs and reels and country-dances ... until at last the little man put down his pipe and turned to the fiddler.

'You're a fine player indeed,' he said, 'and if you come back here in a week and play for a party we'll be having, you'll earn yourself some gold.' Then the little man vanished, leaving the fiddler to stumble home in the dark, thinking about the fairy's request. Gold would be very useful to the poor fiddler ... perhaps the risk would be worth taking. On the other hand, everyone knew it could be dangerous to mix with the Little People. All week he struggled with the decision. Should he stay, should he go? Should he go, should he stay?

A week later the fiddler was playing at another party, and after it finished he made his decision. As he left the gathering to walk to the Fairy Hill, he told a couple of his friends where he was going, and they warned him to be careful. Indeed, they tried to persuade him not to go at all ... but since he insisted, they told him not to eat or drink anything while he was with the Little People, or they would keep him prisoner forever. Eventually the young man promised to let nothing pass his lips that night.

When the fiddler reached the Fairy Hill, there was the little man he'd seen the week before, who handed the fiddler a bag of gold and asked him to start playing. The fiddler put the bag of gold safely in his pocket, and started to play. The little man joined in on his flute, and soon the place was full of fairies, leaping and dancing around the standing stones, in time to the music. Some were beautiful, with the loveliest faces you could imagine. Others had sharp little features, like wild animals, with long, pointed

teeth and fierce smiles. After a couple of hours the fiddler grew
tired and asked for time to rest. The fairies all smiled and nodded,
saying that he'd feel better after a few minutes break and some
food. The Little People fetched golden plates, piled with fruits that
the fiddler had never seen before, and he grew hungry. Forgetting
about his friends' warnings, he reached out his hand, hovering over
the food, deciding which delicious thing to eat first. Suddenly he
noticed a group of pale, shadowy men, just beyond the circle of
dancing fairy folk. Their clothes were old-fashioned, their faces
were lined and troubled, and they were gesturing to him not to eat
any of the food.

Then the fiddler remembered his promise, and was determined
not to touch the food at all, but the fairies grew angry and started
to pull and pinch at him, trying to force him to eat. He picked
up his fiddle and started to play again, distracting the fairies, who
seemed compelled to join in the dancing whenever he played a
tune. Every time he stopped for a rest he was bitten and pinched
and scratched, as the shadowy men looked on from a distance,
shaking their heads, but he still wouldn't touch the food. After
several hours he was exhausted. He stopped to rest again, and this
time the fairies were determined to make him eat. He was such
a wonderful musician that they wanted to keep him with them
forever, to play for them whenever they chose.

They charged at him, knocking the fiddler to the ground,
so that he dropped his violin on to the grass. Then they tried to
force the fruit between his lips, and clamped his nose with their
sharp little fingers, so that he would have to open his mouth
to breathe. He reached out a hand, feeling for his fiddle on
the ground beside him, and plucked at a couple of the strings.
Hearing those notes and thinking he was about to start playing
once more, the fairies released him and leapt into the circle of
stones, preparing to dance again. Suddenly the Little People scattered … the sun had risen over the horizon and their power over
the fiddler was broken.

The fiddler stumbled to his feet and looked around. The fairies
were gone with the darkness, and so were the shadowy men.

He still had his fiddle, he still had his bow, and when he checked his pocket, he still had the bag of gold too. He opened the bag and, sure enough, it was brimming with gold … it hadn't turned to leaves or dust in the morning light, as fairy gold sometimes does. Exhausted, the young man made his way home, fell on to his bed, and slept for hours.

That night his friends came to visit him, to see if he'd survived his encounter with the fairies, and he told them what had happened. 'Lucky you managed to play until dawn,' they said, 'or the Little People would certainly have forced you to eat their food. If even a drop had passed your lips, they would have kept you in the Fairy Kingdom, to play your fiddle for them, forever.'

'But why didn't the shadowy men come to help me?' asked the fiddler. 'Together we could have fought the fairies and escaped.' His friends explained that they thought the shadowy men were humans who had been tricked, just as the fiddler had almost been, into eating fairy food. They were now the fairies' prisoners, and had no power to fight them. The most they had been able to do was to warn the fiddler, so that he didn't fall into the same trap, and that was what they had done.

The fiddler used the gold to buy a cottage and a piece of land, and marry the girl he loved. Then he went back to making his living going around the Island, playing at weddings and funerals and parties, earning a penny here, and a penny there. But from that day on the fiddler always avoided the Fairy Hill, and took the long road home – no matter how tired he was – because he didn't want to get into any more trouble with the fairies.

❧

This tale appears in various forms, and is in *The Green Glass Bottle – Folk Tales from the Isle of Man* by Zena Carus (1975). An older version appears in *The Folklore of the Isle of Man* by A.W. Moore (1891) titled 'The Unfortunate Fiddler'. The following story was recorded by George Waldron, a collector of Manx tales, who lived and worked on the Island from 1720 to 1730:

A fiddler agreed with a stranger that, for so much money, he would play for some company all the twelve days of Christmas. He received some payment in advance but saw his new master vanish into the earth the moment he had made the bargain. No one could be more terrified than was the poor fiddler; he found he had entered himself into the Devil's service and looked upon himself as already damned. Still, having recourse to a clergyman, he felt some hope.

The clergyman told him that, as he had already taken payment, he must go when he was called; but that whatever tunes should be called for, he was to play none but Psalms. On the day appointed, the stranger appeared once more and the fiddler went with him but, obeying the minister's advice, he would only play Psalms. The company to whom he played were so angry that they all vanished at once. The fiddler found himself on the top of a high hill, bruised and hurt, though he could not remember receiving any blows.

THE PHYNODDEREE'S SORROW

Once, long, long ago the Island was a place of magic. There lived the elves and fairies, or as the Island people called them – the Little People. The hero of our story was one such elf.

Like all elves he was handsome beyond compare … but he was also sweet and kind, with a smile on his face, always ready to lend a hand or just give a cheery 'Hello'. But this little elf … he was in love! As he had been roaming the Island one day, he had passed by Glen Aldyn, and there was a little cottage and in that cottage lived a beautiful young maiden. At first the maiden was shy and fearful. The people of the Island did not mix with the little people … it was said to be bad luck … but the little elf was so kind to her, and so charming, that soon they fell deeply in love with one another.

For the elf and the maiden their days passed in a whirlwind of joy and happiness. They would walk hand-in-hand, barefoot on the beach at Laxey harbour, they would have picnics together at the foot of Snaefell Mountain and all the while the little elf would sing for his love, for, I would have you know, all elves have voices sweeter than the morning lark.

But … (and you just knew that there was going be a 'but' somewhere, didn't you?) trouble came when the time of the Harvest Moon came around. Every year all the elves and all the fairies from every corner of the Island gathered together at the fairy court in the Glen of Rushen. It was the time of year that all the Little Folk looked forward to … like Christmas and Easter and weekends and holidays and your birthday all rolled into one! There was much celebrating, but the little elf found that he no longer cared for that anymore. All of the magical wonders of the fairy court were like cheap party tricks compared to the beauty of his lovely maiden. And so he decided that he would much rather spend his time with her than attend the Harvest Moon Festival as he should have done. 'Ohhh … hang the Harvest Moon Festival!' said the little elf out loud when he'd made his decision.

But little did he know that as he said this, another fairy was watching him. This other fairy had taken on the form of a fox cub (for, I would have you know, elves and fairies can change their shape just as easily as you or I would put on a hat and coat!) and, shocked by what he had heard, the fairy ran immediately to tell the grand king of the elves. When the king heard what the little elf had said he was not pleased at all … and shouted, 'WHAT??? How DARE he!' in a voice as loud as thunder.

Angry beyond words, the elf king swore to punish the little elf. So he called upon his great and terrible magic powers to place a hideous curse upon the little elf. He would change the elf's shape and take away the elf's power to change it back! The next day the maiden walked out to the meadow near to her home, to meet with her beautiful elf. Her heart was still light with love and as she waited she sang a little song to herself, but when her love finally appeared he was not as she remembered him at all.

His handsome little body had been changed. He was now huge and hulking and hairy! His once perfect little teeth had become sharp, dirty fangs. And when he spoke and tried to sing to show his maiden that it was him, his voice had become a deep, gruff, grisly growl! He wasn't used to the new shape of his mouth and teeth, so he couldn't make himself understood.

The maiden, although she could see that this creature had once been her lovely elf, was terrified. He was so big and so ugly that she could not bear to look at him. And every time she heard his great growl of a voice it scared her. Finally she could bear it no

more and she ran away, all the way back to her cottage and locked the door. Far behind her, all alone and broken-hearted, was the elf, who, I can now tell you, had been transformed into a creature called a Phynodderee.

The Phynodderee, to try to help him forget his lost love, started to help out the people of the Island. He would cut and gather the hay if he saw a storm coming in, or move big rocks that humans couldn't shift, to help them build their homes.

Sometimes he got a little too enthusiastic. One night, during a terrible snowstorm, the Phynodderee tried to helpfully round up a flock of sheep and get them safely into a barn. The next morning, when he saw the farmer who owned the sheep, the Phynodderee complained that while the whole flock of white sheep had given him no trouble, he'd had to chase the little brown one round the mountain twice before he managed to get her into the barn. This puzzled the farmer, for he had no brown native sheep in his flock. The man went and looked in his barn, and there, amongst the white sheep, was a brown hare, exhausted and asleep after being chased around the mountain all night. The Phynodderee had managed to catch the fastest creature on the Island, thinking, in the darkness, that it was a little brown sheep.

But in the end the Phynodderee discovered all this activity was no use to him! It didn't help him to forget his lovely maiden. And so, one day, the Phynodderee simply disappeared. Some say that he left the Isle of Man in search of a way to change his shape once more and be reunited with his love. And as for the maiden … she too was broken-hearted. Every day and every night she would sit at the cliff's edge looking out to sea, wishing her lovely elf was by her side, and she would quietly cry to herself. Now although the maiden's sobs were as quiet as the whisper of the tiniest mouse, to a fairy's ears they were as loud as ten thousand brass bands all playing at once! And when the elf king heard her he took pity on the poor maid and went to find her. 'Do not weep, fair child,' said the elf king. 'There is no magic that is done that can never be undone! I cannot help your elf, but your love will find a way and when he does, he will return to you. But … we fairies live forever and a day, and you mortals do not. Here, take this charm,' said the elf king handing her an enchanted stone. 'It is my strongest magic. From this moment, you shall not age a single day, nor shall you die, until your love returns to you!'

And so it was! The maiden never grew any older from that day to this. And every single one of those days she would sit by the sea, waiting for the Phynodderee to come home to her. There are people who say that she is still there today! Now you may not believe me, but some say they have seen her on the clifftops at Peel, others on the rocks at Port Erin, still waiting to be reunited with the one she loves!

This version of the story was created by my friend Daniel Jeffrey, for a show we were touring a few years ago – 'Forgotten Fables and Perfidious Pirates' – and is reproduced with his permission. I've been telling this version ever since.

It sticks to the original legend up to the disappearance of the Phynodderee. The reason for him vanishing and the loyal waiting of the Manx maiden are his additions to the story. Not all traditional versions include the elf's love for the Manx maiden, but some certainly do, such as the version told in *The Phynodderee and Other Legends of the Isle of Man* by Edward Callow (1882).

However, in some, the Phynodderee just appears in his hairy troll-like form from the beginning of the tale. This is the case in Sophia Morrison's *Manx Fairy Tales* (1911). Other, more traditional, versions of the tale and the Phynodderee's reasons for disappearing can be found in *The Folklore of the Isle of Man* by A.W. Moore (1891). Moore's version tells how:

> A gentleman, having resolved to build a large house and offices on his property, a little above the base of Snaefell Mountain, at a place called Tholt-e-will, caused the requisite quantity of stones to be quarried on the beach, but one immense block of white stone, which he was very desirous to have for a particular part

of the intended building, could not be moved from the spot, resisted the united strength of all the men in the parish. To the utter astonishment, however, of all, not only this rock, but likewise the whole of the quarried stones, consisting of more than an hundred cart-loads, were in one night conveyed from the shore to the site of the intended homestead by the inde-fatigable *Phynnodderee,* and, in confirmation of this wonderful feat, the white stone is yet pointed out to the curious visitor.

The gentleman for whom this very acceptable piece of work was performed, wishing to remunerate the naked *Phynnodderee,* caused a few articles of clothing to be laid down for him in his usual haunt. The hairy one, on perceiving the habiliments, lifted them up one by one, thus expressing his feelings in Manx:

Bayrn dá'n chione. dy doogh dá'n chione,
Cooat dá'n dreeym, dy doogh dá'n dreeym,
Breechyn dá'n tom, dy doogh dá'n tom,
Agh my she lhiat ooilley, shoh cha nee lhiat Glen reagh Rushen.

Cap for the head, alas! poor head,
Coat for the back, alas! poor back,
Breeches for the breech, alas! poor breech,
If these be all thine, thine cannot be the merry Glen of Rushen.

Having repeated these words, he departed with a melancholy wail, and now:

You may hear his voice on the desert hill
When the mountain winds have power;
'Tis a wild lament for his buried love,
And his long-lost Fairy Bower.

Many of the old people lament the disappearance of the *Phynnodderee,* for they say, 'There has not been a merry world since he lost his ground.'

ONE OF 'THEMSELVES' FOR THE NIGHT

Now there were two brothers, Billy and Tom Beg, who lived in a croft near Dalby. Both of them had been born humpbacked, and they both worked as cobblers, as well as making part of their living from their land and livestock. Billy Beg was the clever one, the pushy one, the bossy one, and he was always telling his brother Tom what to do, and when to do it, and mostly Tom did as he was told.

One day in the autumn, Billy told Tom to go to the mountain, round up their little flock of white sheep, and bring them home before the weather grew harsh. Tom set off, as he'd been asked, and went to the mountain, but he couldn't find their flock. On and on he walked, reluctant to go home without them, partly out of concern for the sheep, and partly because he didn't want to go back and tell his brother that he'd failed. It was now full dark, but the night was fine, and the moon was out, so he could see the path. Eventually he decided to head for home. He'd just have to face his brother's sarcasm and start searching for the sheep again by daylight. Suddenly, however, he found himself surrounded by a grey mist, and before long he lost his way.

When the mist cleared he was in a green glen he'd never seen before, which surprised him considering how well he thought he knew the countryside. In the distance he could hear something or someone coming towards him. It was cheering to think that he would have some company on his journey, but as he listened, and the sound drew nearer, he became puzzled. At first it had sounded like the humming of bees, which is a pleasant and reassuring sound. Then it grew louder, until it sounded like a waterfall, which was not quite so reassuring, since waterfalls don't usually move towards a person. Finally it became like the noise of a great crowd, marching and murmuring ... and Tom began to feel nervous. Out of the darkness appeared the fairy host, with the Little People wearing red caps and riding their horses. They were blowing their horns, waving flags and playing music, and on the ground were lots of little dogs, running around and barking.

Tom Beg gazed at it all in wonder, amazed that he had had the good fortune to see such a splendid sight. As he looked and began to make sense of it all, he realised that he was watching some kind of a rehearsal ... some of the Little Men were practising their drill and battle manoeuvres, others were performing complicated dances and beautiful songs, while the rest were making strange patterns with their flags. One of the Little Fellows spotted Tom, and pointed him out to the grandest of the Little People. This man was dressed in robes of gold and silver, and as he rode towards Tom Beg, Tom bowed as deeply as his humped back allowed. He knew a king when he saw one, and wished to be respectful.

'You've picked a bad time to come this way,' said the king sternly.

'But I'm not here by choice,' said Tom apologetically, 'I got lost. My name's Tom Beg and I'm looking for my sheep.'

'Since you're here,' said the king, more kindly, 'are you one of us for tonight, Tom?'

'Yes,' said Tom, 'I'm happy to be, if you'll have me.'

'Then it will be your duty to take the password. Take up your post at the far end of the glen, and as each regiment goes past, take the password ... let none in or out without it. The password is Monday, Tuesday, Wednesday, Thursday, Friday, Saturday.'

'I'll do that with a heart and a half,' said Tom, proud to be able to help the king of the Little People.

From his viewpoint at the end of the glen, Tom had the pleasure of watching all the Little People rehearsing until the night was almost over. Then the fairy horde got itself in order and marched up the glen towards Tom. The fiddlers led the way, playing their instruments, and the rest marched behind them. As each regiment went past, they gave the password to Tom with a cheery wave, 'Monday, Tuesday, Wednesday, Thursday, Friday, Saturday'. Behind all the rest rode the king, and he too gave the password, 'Monday, Tuesday, Wednesday, Thursday, Friday, Saturday'. Then he nodded his thanks to Tom and summoned one of his men.

'Take the hump from this fellow's back, as a sign of our thanks and goodwill,' ordered the king, and before the words were out of his mouth the hump was whisked off Tom's back and thrown into the hedge. Tom stood up straight with pride, and then made a deep bow to the king. He could bow as deeply as he chose now. He felt like the tallest, straightest man on the Island! When the fairy horde was out of sight, and the sun had risen, he went down the mountain and made his way back to the croft. His heart was light and there was a spring in his step as he walked into the cottage.

Billy Beg was filled with wonder when he saw his brother Tom standing up so straight and strong. He demanded that Tom tell him how the miracle had happened, so Tom explained about meeting the Little People in the glen and watching them practice their drill.

Billy demanded every detail, and insisted that his brother told him again and again, until poor Tom was exhausted. But Billy was the clever one, the pushy one, the bossy one, and he kept on at his brother until he knew every inch of the route Tom had taken, because Billy had a plan.

The next night Billy set off along the mountain road, following the route that Tom had described, and came at last to the green glen. At around midnight he heard distant murmuring, and the thudding of hooves, and into the glen rode the Little People and their king, with their horses and their dogs.

When they saw Billy they all stopped and glared at him, and one of the Little Men came forward and asked his business.

'I am one of Yourselves for the night, and should be glad to do you some service,' said Billy, determined to earn the same reward as his brother.

So he too was told to take the password, 'Monday, Tuesday, Wednesday, Thursday, Friday, Saturday'. The Little Peoples' practice was carried on much as it had been the night before, though Billy took less pleasure in watching it than his brother had. Billy was busy thinking of his reward, and wondering if he could do anything extra to earn some fairy gold in addition … after all, he was the clever one, and he always had to go one better than his brother.

At dawn the regiments rode past Billy, each of them giving him the password, 'Monday, Tuesday, Wednesday, Thursday,

Friday, Saturday'. Last of all came the king with his men, they too gave the password, 'Monday, Tuesday, Wednesday, Thursday, Friday, Saturday'.

'*And Sunday!*' added Billy loudly, thinking himself clever. There was a sharp intake of breath and then a great outcry, for of course Sunday is the Lord's Day, and the Little People didn't wish to be reminded of it. The seventh day was simply not mentioned by them, and they didn't want anybody else referring to it in their presence.

The king was furious and shouted, 'Get the hump that was taken off that fellow's back last night and put it on this man's back' and he pointed to the hump that lay under the hedge.

Before the words were well out of his royal mouth Tom's hump was fixed on to Billy's back.

'Now,' raged the king, his eyes flashing, 'be off, and if ever I find you here again, I will clap another hump on to your front!'

Off marched the fairy horde silent and angry, and left poor Billy standing where they had found him, with a hump growing on each shoulder. He walked home miserably the next morning, trudging down the mountain with a heavy heart and an extra burden on his back. His mood was not improved to discover that Tom was in the best of tempers, having found their little flock of white sheep while his brother was away with the fairies. Tom could sympathise with Billy's frustration so he didn't complain too much when his brother bossed him around, and continued to tell him what to do and when to do it. After all, a brother is a brother, when all's said and done, and they both knew that Billy was the clever one, even if it didn't do him much good in the end.

❧

From *Manx Fairy Tales* by Sophia Morrison (1911). Like the changeling story I've included later on in the book, 'The Fairy Child', I'm a little uncomfortable about this tale because of the way it portrays disability … but it is a traditional tale of its time, and deserves to be included in this collection, in that context.

THE SILVER CUP

There was once a farmer living in the south of the Island, and his cows were the best cows in the area. Nowhere could you see such a fine herd of cattle … seriously, if you were into cows, you would have been impressed with his. He certainly was … they were the pride of his heart, and they provided him with plenty of milk and butter.

But after a while he began to think that something was wrong with the cows. He went to the cowshed first thing every morning, and generally the cows were bright of eye and full of milk. Then one morning he noticed the cows looking so tired that they could hardly stand. When it came to milking time the poor creatures hadn't a drop of milk to give. This happened morning after morning and the farmer became terribly worried. He started to think that someone had put an evil eye on his cows, so he swept up some of the dust from the crossroads close by, in a shovel, and sprinkled it on their backs. If witchcraft was involved, this should have undone it … but the cows got no better. So he wondered if someone was coming after dark to steal the milk. He decided to sit in the cowshed and keep watch all one night to see if he could catch the thief.

So, after everyone had gone to bed, he crept out of the house and hid himself under some straw in a corner of the cowshed. Hour after hour he stayed hidden in the dark, but he heard nothing except for the cows' breathing and the rustling of their straw. He was getting very cold and stiff, and he had pretty much decided to give up and go into the house to get warm.

Suddenly he noticed a glimmering light under the door and he began to hear things … bustling, muttering, chattering things! The cowshed door opened and in came a whole troupe of Little Men, dressed in green coats with leather caps on their heads. Peeking through the straw, the farmer saw that their hunting horns hung by their sides, their whips were in their hands, and scores of tiny fairy dogs of every colour – green, blue, yellow, scarlet, and all the other hues you can think of – leapt and danced around their feet. The cows were lying down and the Little Men loosened the yokes from the cows' necks, then they hopped on the animals' backs, about a dozen Little Men on each cow, and cracked their short whips. The cows jumped to their feet and galloped off, with the hunters on their backs, and the fairy dogs running along the ground after them.

The farmer ran into the stable, got on his horse and gave chase. The night was dark but he could hear the click of the cows' hoofs on the stones, and the sound of the little fairy dogs barking carried on the night air. He heard, too, the laughing of Themselves, and all these sounds helped him to follow the hunt on horseback, even though he couldn't see them in the darkness.

On and on they went, over hedges and over ditches till they got to the Fairy Hill, and the farmer was still following close on their heels. On any other night he would not have gone within a mile of the great green mound, but he had to keep following his beloved cows. When the Little Fellows came to the hill they sounded their horns. The hill opened, bright light streamed out, and the farmer heard sounds of music and merriment coming from within. The Little People passed through, and the farmer slid off his horse and slipped in unnoticed after them. The hill seemed to almost close behind them and he found himself in a fine room, lit up till it was brighter than a summer's day. The whole place was crowded with Little People, young and old, men and women, all decked out for a ball. It was the grandest ballroom he had ever seen, not that he'd seen many, but even if he had, few could have matched the finery of that room, or of the clothing of the Little People who had gathered that night to celebrate. Among the people in the room, he noticed some faces that he thought he had seen before, but he took no notice of them nor they of him. He was more interested in watching the dancing, which was like the dancing of flowers in the wind, full of grace but with a wild energy about it … the kind of dancing he had never seen before.

In another part of the room, the farmer was horrified to see some of his cows were being killed and roasted. He almost cried out in protest, but he didn't dare draw attention to himself. Surely Themselves would punish an uninvited guest? And there were so many of them that they could easily overpower him, if they chose to. He sighed to see poor Daisy and Bluebell, and Ivy too, meeting such an unexpected and sudden end, but he kept silent.

After the dance there was a great feast, with scores of tables set out with silver and gold, and wonderful things to eat and drink, all of the very best quality. As the guests took their places at one of the tables, a man, whose face the farmer thought he knew, whispered to him, 'Don't eat or drink anything while you're here, or you'll become like me, and never be able to go home again.' He looked around at the food spread upon the table. The roast beef held no appeal for him, but the plates were piled with delicacies, foods he had never seen before and couldn't put a name to. It was all very tempting, but he made himself think of his wife and his family. The wish to see them again outweighed his hunger and curiosity, and he didn't touch a crumb. He looked round, trying to spot the fellow who had warned him, to thank him for the advice, but the man had vanished.

When the feast was coming to an end there was a shout for the Stirrup Cup. Someone ran to fetch it so that they could all drink a toast. The one among the Little People who seemed to be their king, filled it with red wine, took a sip himself, and passed it on to the rest. It was going round from one to another until it came to the farmer, who saw, when he had it in his hands, that it was of fine carved silver, and more beautiful than anything he'd ever seen outside that place. He thought to himself, 'The Little Folk have stolen, killed and eaten my cattle. This cup is very valuable, and worth more than the price of the cows they've taken. It would only be fair for me to keep it, to compensate me for all I've lost.' So standing up and grasping the silver cup tightly in his hand, he held it up and said: 'Shoh Slaynt!' Which is the Manx toast, meaning 'Here's health!'

Then he threw the cupful of wine over Themselves and the lights. In an instant the place was plunged into darkness, save for a sliver of grey pre-dawn light, which came through the chink of the partly closed door. The farmer made for it, cup in hand, slammed the door behind him and ran for his life.

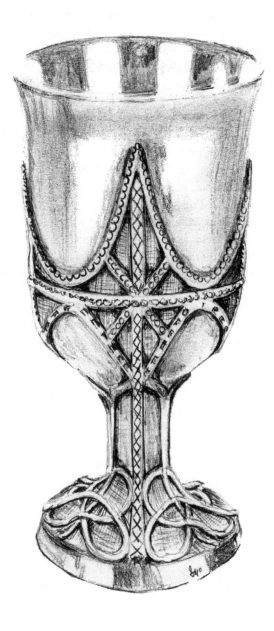

After a moment of uproar Themselves poured out of the hill after him, in full chase. The farmer, who had a good start, ran as he had never run before. He was sure he would get little mercy at their hands if he was caught, so he kept off the stepping stones, and went splashing through the wet mire instead, for he knew they could not capture him in the water. He looked over his shoulder and caught a glimpse of the whole Mob Beg behind him, close at his heels, but he ran in the water till he came to the churchyard, and they could not touch him there either.

Now that he was safe on holy ground the farmer could finally get his breath back, and settled down to wait until dawn, when he knew the Little People would be gone. Once the sun came up, the exhausted man made his way home. The first place he went, of course, was to his cowshed, and there he found the rest of his cows. They were worn out from the adventures of the night, and gave no milk that morning, but after that the Little People left the herd alone, and soon they recovered, and went back to being fine healthy providers of milk once more.

As for the cup … he decided that it was wiser not to try and sell it, for all that he needed to buy more cows. He feared that exchanging it for money might make the Little People even angrier. He took advice, and was told that the only safe use for an enchanted cup was as a chalice for communion wine. So he put the silver cup in the church at Rushen, where all could enjoy and benefit from it, but its holy setting would keep it from causing any harm. They did say though, that after his narrow escape from Themselves that night, the farmer never dared to go out of his house after dark again … in case the Little People were waiting for him.

∾

Versions of this story appear in *The Folklore of the Isle of Man* by A.W. Moore (1891), and in *Manx Fairy Tales* by Sophia Morrison (1911).

∾

THE LOST WIFE

There was once a farmer who was married to a beautiful young woman. He loved her very much, because not only was she lovely to look at, but she was kind and funny as well. When the farmer was out working in the fields, he would daydream about his darling wife, and look forward to going home to her. His wife adored him too, and although they both had to work hard on the farm, she would always try to find the time to bake him his favourite cakes and puddings ... he had a bit of a sweet tooth, her husband. Every day they would try to bring a smile to each other's faces, and took pleasure in simply being together.

Then one day, everything changed. His wife was beside him in the bed when he went to sleep, but when the farmer woke up in the morning, she was gone. There had been a storm in the night, and he half remembered her saying that she was going to go and check that the hen house door hadn't blown open. The chickens were her pride and joy, and she didn't want some nasty fox getting them. He had gone back to sleep, expecting to find her beside him in the morning, but there was no sign of her. He searched their farmhouse, and then the farm, and then asked everyone in the village, but she seemed to have disappeared without a trace. He searched further afield, from the Point of Ayr in the north to the Calf of Man in the south, but no one could tell him anything. They could speculate though, as people do. Some folks said she must be dead, and others suggested that she had been taken by the Little People, but nobody actually knew what had happened to her. The farmer waited and waited for several years but she never came back.

Eventually he married again ... a woman who had set her cap at him and was determined to have him for a husband, for the farm was doing nicely, and being the farmer's wife, well, that was a fine position to marry into. He was fond of his new wife, but not in the way he had adored his first bride. They got along well enough, she had brought some money with her as a dowry and money is always welcome, but somehow he kept on thinking about the girl he had loved.

Then one night, when the farmer was out in his barn, attending to a sick calf, his first wife appeared before him. She was as lovely as ever, but she seemed troubled. She kept looking over her shoulder, nervously, as she spoke.

'Husband, my husband,' she whispered, 'I was kidnapped by the Little People, and I'm being held a prisoner not far away from here. I can be set free, if you will do as I ask.'

'I'll do anything to have you in my arms once more,' said the farmer. 'Just tell me what you need me to do.'

'The Little People will be riding though this barn at midnight on Friday. It's Midsummer's Eve and the faerie hordes will be setting out on their Wild Hunt. We'll be going in one door and out of the other, and I'll be on horseback behind one of the Little Men. Before then you must sweep the barn clean of straw … not a single piece must be left behind. Then when we ride through, catch hold of my bridle rein, hang on to it tightly, and I shall be set free.' She smiled at him, and then vanished into thin air, as suddenly as she had appeared. He heard a sound, just outside the door, but when he raced over to look, no one was there.

That Friday the farmer spent the whole day in the barn sweeping up all the straw, searching everywhere to make sure he hadn't missed a single piece. Then he crept into a corner of the barn and waited, silently, in the dark. Sure enough, at midnight the barn doors burst open, and in rode a company of Little People. Their jackets were green and their caps were red, and their horses were the finest he had ever seen. Sweet music filled the air as they cantered into the building. On the last horse sat his lovely wife, still young, and very beautiful, her arms around the waist of one of the Little Men as he guided the horse through the barn. The farmer leapt out of hiding and grabbed the bridle rein, but the horse didn't stop. Instead it shook its head from side to side, and the farmer was flung this way and that way, while the little man beat at him with a riding crop. However hard he tried, the farmer couldn't keep hold of the bridle rein. The horse, now free of him, raced for the other door, and as they rode out through it, his first wife pointed towards a barrel in the corner, and called out softly,

'A straw has been put under that barrel. That's why you couldn't hold on to me. Now we're lost to each other forever.'

The farmer turned and saw his second wife crouched behind the barrel that the girl had pointed to. The woman had overheard his conversation with his first wife a few nights before, and was determined not to be pushed out by the return of the farmer's beloved bride. It was her he had heard outside the barn door that night, eavesdropping, and it was she who had deliberately slipped a single straw under the barrel, after the farmer had checked the barn was clear for the final time. Her triumphed was short-lived though, for all fondness between them died that night ... and eventually she returned to her own family, leaving the farmer alone. And alone he remained, for after the Little People galloped away that night, the young wife was never seen, or heard of, again.

∽

This is another story from Sophia Morrison's *Manx Fairy Tales* (1911).

THE FAIRY BRIDGE

On the road from Douglas to the south of the Island, there is a bridge over the River Santon, which is known to everyone on the Island as the Fairy Bridge. Few Manx people cross it without calling out a greeting to the Little People, and visitors are encouraged to do the same, for good luck. The trees beside the bridge are usually hung with ribbons, and pieces of paper asking Themselves for help and blessings, and giving thanks for luck and success. With nowhere to park anywhere near the bridge, apart from on the narrow road itself, attaching these wishes requires both daring and a good deal of fairy protection.

Although not everyone claims to believe in the Little People these days, they don't want to get on the wrong side of them either. Calling out a greeting is supposed to bring good fortune, while failing to make this polite gesture exposes you to the annoyance of

Themselves and bad luck. This could be anything from a flat tyre to a bad accident, and most people don't want to risk it, just in case.

During the Second World War there was a Fleet Air Arm base in the south of the Island. There is a story that the commanding officer heard that the pilots, as they crossed the bridge, would salute, as an acknowledgement of the Little People. He considered this to be barbaric and superstitious, and posted an order that the practice had to stop, and it did.

Over the next two weeks a couple of aircraft were mysteriously lost over the Irish Sea, and in the end the commanding officer revoked the order. The pilots went back to saluting the

Little People when they crossed the bridge, and the planes were safe in the air once more.

An even older story about the bridge is from the 1930s, when an Englishman bought a farm nearby and announced that he was going to grow corn in a field that contained a fairy ring. Local people were worried, as they said that this field was where the Little People danced under the harvest moon. They asked the farmer to leave it be ... but in his opinion it had lain fallow for long enough already.

He sewed the corn and looked to have a good harvest from the crop, but the night before it was due to be mown something unusual happened. The countryside was filled with strange noises, although the weather on the rest of the Island was calm. In the morning the corn was battered and bruised and not worth harvesting, and in the middle of the field was a perfect circle, where the corn seemed to have been trodden flat into the ground by hundreds of little dancing feet.

Where such a tradition as the Fairy Bridge comes from is difficult to pin down. Some say that it isn't even the 'true' Fairy Bridge, which is on an old pack road that crosses a stream further north. However, the River Santon may carry fairy tradition along a good stretch of its length. It was once the dividing line between the lands of Rushen Abbey and those of the Lord of Mann. Anyone fleeing justice, and hoping to seek sanctuary with the monks, would be likely to say a prayer of thanks as they forded the river and set foot on Church land, where the Lord of Mann's justice couldn't touch them. This tribute of prayer and thankfulness was gradually altered, when the historical details started to fade, into calling out a greeting to the Little People, which is much more in keeping with Manx tradition.

꙰

From *Fables, Fantasies and Folklore of the Isle of Man* by Harry Penrice (1996), *The Folklore of the Isle of Man* by Margaret Killip (1975) and *The Most Amazing Places of Folklore & Legend in Britain* by Reader's Digest Association (2011).

THE FAIRY CHILD

There was once a woman who lived near Glen Maye, and she didn't know what to do. She had a child that had fallen sick and she was in great distress.

It seems that when the child was about a fortnight old, and a fine healthy baby, he was left asleep while the mother went to the well for water. Now the woman forgot to put the tongs on the cradle, to protect the child and keep the Little People away, for they hate cold iron. When the mother came back the child was crying pitifully, and there was no quieting him. And from that very hour the flesh seemed to melt off his bones till he became as ugly and as shrivelled a child as you could imagine. For the next four years he lay in his cradle without ever attempting to walk or to speak. He howled and whined day and night, and she never got a moment's rest, though she did her best to care for him lovingly. Then one day in spring, Hom Beg Bridson, the tailor, was in the house sewing. He was a terribly clever fellow, for he was always travelling from house to house tailoring, and gathering wisdom as he went.

Well, when he'd passed the house on previous journeys, the tailor had noticed the child's bad behaviour. When the woman was there the babe would lie in his cot, crying and screaming, but if the mother was out feeding the cows and pigs, the baby would lift his head up out of the cradle, haul himself upright and pull faces.

That day the woman wanted to go to the shop to sell some eggs, and she asked the tailor to keep an eye on the child as he sat by her fire, sewing. When she was gone the tailor began to whistle a hymn tune to himself as he stitched.

'Stop that, Hom Beg,' said a little harsh voice. The tailor was taken by surprise, and looked round to see who had spoken. 'Stop that dreary church music,' said the child, 'and give us a cheerful tune.'

'Anything to oblige,' said Hom, whistling a jig. 'That's a fine tune that you're whistling,' commented the child, 'can you dance to it?'

'Indeed I can,' said Hom, 'can you, my lad? I'd like to see you dance … but I don't suppose you can, you being so sick and all!'

The tailor was hoping to trick the child, for he was sure now that the little fella was one of Themselves.

'Then take down the fiddle hanging on the wall, and play the tune of "The Big Wheel", and you'll see if I can dance or not,' said the child, with a wicked grin.

The tailor lifted the instrument down and began to tune it, but before he could start playing the little fella asked Hom to clear some space in the kitchen, so that there was enough room for dancing. Hom did as he was asked, and then began to play. As soon as the music started, the child leapt out of the cradle and began to spin and twirl around the kitchen, shouting, 'More power to your elbow Hom, keep playing the fiddle.'

Hom played faster and faster, till the lad was jumping as high as the table. Up leapt the child on to the dresser, and higher yet on to the mantelpiece. Next the child began to dance so fast that he was almost flying around the room, kicking out against the walls to turn in the air and change direction. This whirling jig made Hom feel dizzy just watching him and finally he threw down the fiddle and said, 'You're not the child that was in the cradle!'

'True enough,' said the little fella, 'for I'm not a child at all. Now keep playing. Four years I've been lying there bored, and I'm ready to have some fun.'

At that moment they heard the mother's footstep outside the door and the child jumped back in the cradle. 'Get on with your sewing, Hom, don't say a word,' said the little fella, covering himself up with his blanket till nothing could be seen of him except his eyes, which peeked out like a ferret's.

When the mother came into the house, the tailor, all of a tremble, was sitting cross-legged on the floor, pretending to be busy sewing. The child in the cradle was grinning and crying as usual.

'Why on earth is everything shoved all over the place, Hom?' asked the woman. Going over to the child she said gently, 'Did you think I'd forgotten you? I know it's time for your dinner, and I'll fetch it straight away.' The tailor had been wondering what to do for the best, for he was scared of upsetting the Little People by telling their secret, but seeing the exhausted woman's kindly face decided him. She had toiled for four years to care for a child who wasn't what she thought … and she had to know the truth.

'Look here, woman,' said the tailor. 'Never mind about his food. Go and fetch a stack of good turf and a bundle of fern.' The woman looked puzzled, but she knew Hom had a reputation as a wise man, so she trusted him, and did as he asked.

She brought the turf, and threw a bundle of fern on it. The tailor began to build up the fire until it was burning so fiercely that the woman thought the chimney would catch alight. Then he added the fern on top and the room began to fill with smoke. The child was watching the tailor in horror, wondering what he was going to do next, and his whining changed into a call that sounded like 'Come and get me, come and get me!'

'Time to send you home,' said Hom, reaching out as if to lift the little fella up and throw him on to the blazing turf fire. Before the tailor was able to lay a hand on him, the child leaped out of the cradle and headed for the door, while the mother watched in amazement.

Then the door flew open with a bang and the little fella shot out of it. There was a great noise outside, of running feet, laughter and greetings, and the tailor and the mother ran to see what was going on. All they could see was a flock of low-lying clouds shaped like gulls chasing each other away up the glen. The mother was heartbroken. She knew now that the Little People had taken her own sweet child and left a changeling in his place, but she had done her best to care for the creature, and grown fond of it after a fashion, and now it too was gone.

As she and Hom turned to go back inside the cottage, she saw her own sweet, rosy, smiling child, sitting on the grass. He was four years older than when she had last seen him, but she knew in her heart that this was her own child, returned to her by the Little People, and she was filled with all the joy in the world.

I have to admit to being a little uncomfortable with changeling tales, because the genuine belief in changelings in the past sometimes led to cruelty to real children who had health issues or disabilities and failed to thrive. Some parents, convinced that these were change-lings, treated them harshly in order to get the fairies to come and retrieve their child and return the healthy human one. Of course … outside of fairy stories … that didn't happen. Thankfully such cases were very rare, but they did occur sometimes.

Since the belief in fairies stealing children was strong, people devised a number of ways to protect babies, especially before they were baptised, when the children were thought to be at their most vulnerable. Salt was meant to deter fairies, as was iron, so pokers and other implements would be left with unat-tended children to keep them safe. Another protective measure, both for human beings and animals, was to have a piece of the mountain ash, in the form of a cross, made without a knife, put over the threshold of their dwellings.

This tale appears in both *The Folklore of the Isle of Man* by A.W. Moore (1891) and *Manx Fairy Tales* by Sophia Morrison (1911), under the title 'The Fairy Child of Close-ny-Lheiy'.

THE FAIRY SADDLE

The Little People on the Isle of Man don't spend their time flit-tering about on glittery wings. Oh no, these are creatures of the earth, and they enjoy earthly pursuits … like riding. And when I say riding, I don't mean taking a gentle hack along the lanes. They like *speed*, riding as fast and as far as they can, leaping over hedges, soaring over stone walls, and most of all, they love to hunt.

Now looking after a horse is hard work, and on the whole, the Little People aren't into hard work. Why should they bother when there are horses in the fields that they can ride whenever they choose, and it's the humans who take care of them? People ride during the day and, of course, the Little People ride at night, so it's rare for the owner of the horse to even know what's going on. However, that doesn't mean that they never guess. If a horse is found in his stall wet with perspiration, and no particular reason can be found, it is said that he must have been ridden by the fairies.

Now there is a story about this superstition, with solid evidence to back it up. Very solid evidence … solid as a rock, in fact.

Once upon a time the vicar of Braddan, who was an old man, was terribly worried. His horse was disappearing from its field at night, but would be back in the morning, covered in sweat and completely exhausted, as if he'd been ridden at speed for many miles.

This troubled the vicar in two ways. Firstly, the horse wasn't young and the old man was worried that all this exertion might be too much for the creature. Secondly, the vicar often needed to ride the horse himself at night, if he was called out to someone in need on the other side of the parish. As often as not, he would go to saddle his horse only to find it gone from the field. Then the elderly vicar would have to walk to the parishioner, arriving there late and exhausted. He was convinced that this strange disappearing act wasn't doing himself, or the horse, any good.

Despite asking everyone in the neighbourhood if they had any idea who was stealing his horse, he could never find out who was responsible. Some people did think it might have been the Little People, but they didn't like to suggest that … not to the vicar. They knew his views on the mystical creatures of the Island, and that he would gently point out that belief in such things was all superstitious nonsense. The poor old man was losing sleep over it, however, wondering if he had an enemy somewhere, who was doing this to spite him, though in truth he was a kind and gentle man, and nobody who knew him would ever hurt a hair on his head. He tried to tell himself that if someone in the village had need of his horse, who was he to begrudge it to them … but did they need to ride the poor creature so hard?

One sleepless night there was a hammering at the door. He opened it to find a young boy, who'd come to ask the vicar to go with him quickly, to his grandmother's house. The old woman was dying, and asking for the vicar to come and administer

the Sacrament to her, so that she could pass in peace. The vicar grabbed his coat and his bag and hurried after the lad. The old lady lived in the village, so he didn't need his horse, but as he passed the field he could see that the poor creature was missing once again.

However, when he reached the old lady's cottage any thoughts of the horse were pushed to the back of his mind as he comforted her, prayed with her, and gave her the last Sacrament. Then he spent some time with the bereaved family before heading back towards his home, just as the dawn was beginning to break. As he neared the field where he kept his horse, he observed a little man in a green jacket, with a riding whip in his hand, approaching rapidly on horseback.

The horse he was riding, of course, was the vicar's. The little man leapt down and was soon turning the horse loose in the field, having obviously ridden it hard all night. The little fellow removed the horse's saddle and threw it down beside the low stone wall that was built around the field, before taking the bridle off the exhausted creature. Then the little man turned round to lift the saddle and return it to its usual place. At that moment he saw the vicar watching him open-mouthed, and vanished instantly into thin air.

The saddle turned to stone, still in the shape of a saddle, and has remained so ever since. Though the wall has been built up higher since, the Saddlestone still sticks out of it, and can be seen on Saddlestone Road, just outside Douglas. Needless to say, the old vicar's horse was never 'borrowed' again. He said prayers of gratitude to God, but he also stopped telling the villagers that belief in the Little People was just superstitious nonsense. He had to really. How could he deny their existence, when he had seen one of them for himself?

This story is in A.W. Moore's *The Folklore of the Isle of Man* (1891), as well as cropping up in guidebooks, and the Saddlestone really can still be seen, on what is now called Saddle Road, just off Peel Road.

THE FAIRY SWEETHEART

Now the lhiannan shee is a fairy sweetheart, which sounds enchanting, doesn't it? But as with any situation where humans get mixed up with the Little People, there's always a price to pay. The fairy sweetheart is beautiful, she is charming, and she seeks the love of human men. Well, when I say love, perhaps I really mean besotted devotion … there are no half measures with the lhiannan shee. She particularly seeks out artists and poets … for she loves to be their muse. This *can* mean that they are inspired by her, their creative work becomes incredible, and everyone admires them … but not for long. The fairy sweetheart feeds on their life, and the young men waste away … often going mad before they die.

Like the young man who lived near Port Erin hundreds of years ago. He was being followed around by a lhiannan shee and he noticed her … she didn't like being noticed by just anybody. She preferred to pick and choose her own 'victims', so she sent him mad. Before long he was sleeping out in the barn and talking to his fairy sweetheart all night ... though by day he was silent. Nobody knew what to do with him, but they didn't have to worry for long ... his beloved sucked the life out of him within a couple of months, and he withered away and died.

Now with a creature as dangerous as a lhiannan shee, you can understand people going out of their way to avoid her attention. After all, who would want a fairy sweetheart who intended to suck you dry and send you mad? Well, the odd writer, maybe, or a painter, or poet ... those who aspired to greatness and hoped a fairy sweetheart would help them achieve it ... if you could just overlook the downsides of the relationship ... and the short-lived nature of the fame she brought them. Suffice to say that any sane person would avoid coming into contact with a lhiannan shee, if they possibly could.

Now long ago in the parish of Bradden, there was a great house called Kirkby, though nothing remains of the building these days except its site, part of which is now the picturesque churchyard of Old Braddan church, with its numerous carved stone crosses.

It seemed the household from Kirkby must have had concerns about a lhiannan shee latching on to somebody in their family. Was it that they saw one loitering about, waiting to ensnare their firstborn son? Or perhaps one of the men in the house was an artist or a writer, and especially vulnerable to such a creature? Or maybe the family had such a high sense of their own importance that they felt that out of everyone in the district, a lhiannan shee was *bound* to pick on them? Whatever the cause, they wanted to find a way to prevent it happening and protect the family down through the generations ... and they did!

First they decided that they needed something special, to dedicate to the lhiannan shee. They looked amongst all their possessions, but nothing was good enough. Then they heard of a beautiful cup said to have belonged to Magnus, the Norwegian King of Man, who took it from the shrine of St Olave. Surely such an object would be special enough? Of course, when it came up for sale it was terribly expensive, and the family even had to sell some of their lands to acquire it.

Once they got their hands on this cup they had to do a deal with the fairy sweetheart. You see, the mother of this family had indeed seen a lhiannan shee hanging about the gardens and woods that surrounded their property, and she had reason to be worried. She herself had had a brother and lost him to just such a creature … he had died young, enthralled by his fairy sweetheart, even as the life was sucked out of him. Now this mother feared for her son. He was still just a little too young for the creature to enslave him, but it wouldn't be long before he was old enough to be in danger … and the lhiannan shee was waiting.

This young man was their only son … and heir to their lands and property. His sisters, and he had several, could not inherit any of it, in terms of what the law allowed, so the family had double the reason to want to keep him safe. Every night for weeks the mother watched at the window, and eventually saw a figure moving in the shadows, beneath the young man's window. The fairy sweetheart was preparing to attract the young man's interest and begin to cast her spell on him. The mother, who had the courage of a lion, strode out towards the creature, taking the remarkable cup with her.

'I know what you want,' remarked the mother, when she reached the creature's side. 'You want love and admiration, and to be kept in people's thoughts constantly.'

'What of it?' replied the fairy sweetheart, tall and beautiful in the moonlight. 'I can have what I want from any man I choose. I don't need to bother talking with an old crone like you.'

'Ah,' said the mother wisely, 'but you can only be loved by one man at a time, and only while they live … wouldn't you rather be honoured by a whole family, down through the years? To be thought of as a peaceful spirit, and admired, rather than hated?'

There was a long pause, while the creature thought, then she asked, 'How would I achieve that?'

The mother smiled, 'Allow us to dedicate this cup to you as our peaceful spirit. We will drink a toast to you on special occasions, and remember you in our hearts with gratitude, throughout the year and down the generations.'

The fairy reached out and took the cup, inspecting it closely. It was large and made of crystal, and engraved with a pattern of floral scrolls and upright pillars. It was ancient and a thing of beauty, and the lhiannan shee acknowledged it as such. She handed it back to the mother asking, 'What would I have to do to receive this tribute ... this fond remembrance?'

'All we ask is that you leave my son alone, and all the sons of this house, down the generations, for as long as we remember to acknowledge you.'

'Very well,' agreed the fairy. 'But if you should forget, or shatter this cup, I will haunt the men of this house, down those same generations, forever.'

And so it was that the cup was passed down through the family, only being used once a year, at Christmas, when the Lord of the Manor drank a toast from it to the lhiannan shee ... the peaceful spirit of his home and hearth. Many years later, when that family merged with the Fletchers, it became known as 'The Ballafletcher Drinking Glass', and the tradition continued down the ages, until the family gradually died out ... of *natural* causes.

This comes from *The Folklore of the Isle of Man* by A.W. Moore (1891). The Ballafletcher Drinking Glass still exists, and can be seen on display in the Manx Museum in Douglas, in the Folklore Section of the Social History Gallery.

THE LOST SHEEP

Sometimes the Little People seem set on making mischief for everyone, but that's not always how they behave. To be fair, they can be kind as well ... and because everyone wanted to keep on the right side of the Little People, there were quite a few traditions that built up around keeping them happy. One was to keep the fire burning in the house all night, so that Themselves might come in and enjoy it. It was also the custom to fill a bowl with clean water for them before going to bed. This water was never used for anything else, and was thrown out in the morning. The women, too, would not spin on Saturday evenings, as this was thought to displease the Mooinjer-Veggey, the Little People. Every time bread was baked a small bit of dough was stuck on the wall for the Little People to eat ... and if butter was churned a little of that was left out for them too. Perhaps because of this, sometimes a woman might get up to find that a few of her household chores had been done for her, or the Little People would find other ways to repay kindness with kindness.

But, if anyone was rash enough not to follow these traditions, or to abuse the Little People in any way, they would be sure to suffer for it ... perhaps they would get ill, or their crops wouldn't grow, or visitors to the Island might find that the weather would be bad, just when they hoped it would be fine.

One thing you can be pretty sure of though, is that the Little People enjoy a good story ... doesn't everybody? And that was something Billie was good at. And because he told his stories so well, Themselves would sometimes listen in, while Billie told his tales to his friends. He made his living by doing odd jobs here and there, though they didn't always go smoothly ... like the time that he and his brother agreed a fee to fell a dozen large trees in a field that ran beside the road in Ramsey. The job was for the owner of the field, one of the rich men of the area, and it was hard work, especially since they were supposed to get the trees up roots and all. They laboured for several days, and were exhausted, but when they had dug around the final tree, a great wind rose and pushed the last tree over, pulling the roots clear of the ground. The brothers were delighted that luck was on their side for once, but when they went to claim the money they'd agreed, the landowner refused to pay them the full amount, saying that they'd been 'helped by God'. Billie and his brother were furious.

'Helped by God?' he muttered. 'If I could contact the Devil himself, I'd get *his* help, alright ... to put every tree back in the ground, roots and all!' When the Little People heard him telling that tale, they chuckled with delight.

Well, Billie's family was one of the ones that always did right by the Little People, and he quite often caught a glimpse of them around his home. He heard them singing too sometimes, which he claimed was the loveliest sound in the world. Now Billie could tell a good tale, and perhaps he exaggerated now and then, for none of us are perfect, but he did care about the little flock of sheep he had on the family's patch of land, and he looked after them well. One day his favourite ewe went missing … he searched everywhere he could think of, but couldn't find any trace of the animal. For two nights he fretted about her, wondering where she'd got to, but eventually he had to leave off looking.

He'd agreed to go into Ramsey with his sister Mary Ellen, and help her carry the groceries home. They were walking back when Mary suddenly remembered that she had to call in on a friend for a few minutes, so Billie said he'd wait for her further along the road. He walked up the lane until he came to a little stand of trees. The light was fading fast, and he lay down under the trees to wait. When he looked up into the branches, he saw the little fellas, as he called them, in little blue coats and little red caps, leaping and skipping through the branches. There were several of them, and he could see their faces clearly for there was a bit of a moon. Well, you might not think that you'd fall asleep under such circumstances, but Billie was tired. He been searching for and worrying about his missing sheep for two nights and he *might* have had a drop or two of ale while his sister was doing the shopping.

Whatever the reason, he slept, and the little people came down to the ground to talk to him. While he was asleep they whispered to him where to find his missing sheep, though when he woke up, they were gone. After his sister caught up with him, they took the road home, and once the house was in sight, Billie asked her to deal with the groceries, saying he had to go and have one last look for his missing sheep. He was hoping the Little People had been telling him the truth about where the ewe might be, unless he had dreamt the whole thing. He headed up the Glebe, through the woods, and began to search along the hedgerow. Sure enough, there in a hollow, which he hadn't noticed during his earlier search, was the sheep, stuck in a thorn bush, in the very place that the Little People had told him she would be.

Whether they'd helped him in return for his family's kindness, or because they enjoyed his stories, Billie neither knew nor cared. He'd got his lost sheep back, and that was good enough for him.

༄

This is from *Legends of a Lifetime* by George E. Quayle (1979).

5

THE BIG FOLK

THE GIANT AND THE BUGGANE

Finn MacCooil was an Irish giant, and the buggane was a Manx
goblin-like creature that could take any size and shape it chose,
including that of a giant. Now, Finn came across from the
Mountains of Mourne to see what the Isle of Man was like, since
he could see it from Ireland. Well, he was bound to be curious,
having helped to make the Island by throwing the land into the
sea during his battle with a fellow giant, wasn't he? Finn liked the
Isle of Man so much that he decided to stay for a while, living
down at Cregneash. The buggane had heard all about Finn
MacCooil, so he came down from the top of Barrule to have a look
at him. Finn knew that the buggane would want to pick a fight,
to see who was the stronger, and Finn did not feel like fighting that
day. 'Leave him to me,' said Finn's wife, 'I'll deal with him!'

Before long they caught sight of the buggane, and he was a
walking terror. He had chosen a huge and hideous shape for his visit
to the giant, and he was racing down towards them from Barrule.

'Slip into the cradle, Finn,' said his wife, pointing to the cot she
had insisted on Finn building for her, for she was longing for a
child of her own, and wished to be prepared. 'Wrap this around
yourself, and leave the talking to me!'

Finn grabbed the sheet his wife had handed him, slipped off his
clothes, and wrapped the huge piece of cloth around his middle

like a giant nappy, then squeezed himself into the cradle. Moments
later they could hear the buggane hammering at the door.

'Where's Himself?' said the buggane, flinging the door open.

'He's not at home just now,' replied Finn's wife, calmly. 'Do you
want to wait for him?'

'I'm in no rush,' answered the buggane, 'I might as well wait,'
and he sat down in Finn's chair.

'Please yourself,' said the woman, 'but I must get on with my
baking.' The buggane leaned back in the giant's chair, making
himself at home, and glanced around the room.

'Who have you got in the cradle?' asked the creature.

'That's our baby,' said Finn's wife, trying not to smile.

'In the name of the Unknown Powers, what sort of a man is
Himself, if that's the size of his baby?'

'Oh, Finn's a big and powerful man, and the child takes after his
father, though at the moment he's little enough, just a few months
old. He's a lot of growing to do yet, if he's going to be as big as Finn,'

said the giant's wife, casually. She was baking barley bread, and when it was cooked, she slipped the griddle iron in between two portions of bread when the buggane wasn't looking, and gave it to the creature to eat, with a quart of buttermilk. He went to try and munch on it, but he couldn't take even a single bite, because of the metal hidden in it. Indeed, he feared he'd broken a tooth the bread seemed so tough.

'What kind of bread is it?' complained the buggane. 'I've never tasted anything as hard as this.'

'It's the sort I'm giving to Finn,' she said. 'He won't eat anything else … he reckons most bread is so soft it's not worth the eating.'

By now Finn had cottoned on to his wife's plan, so he got up out of the cradle and began to roar for a piece of bread, as a child might. She fetched him a clout on the ear, saying, 'Stop your noise, and stand up straight.' Then she handed 'the baby' a big lump of the bread, adding, 'Eat, eat … tuck into that, and don't leave any of it. I can't abide waste.'

The buggane leapt up in protest, saying, 'He'll break his teeth, woman! He can't eat bread as hard as that.'

'Of course he can,' said Finn's wife proudly and 'the baby' chomped up the whole piece of bread (for his piece, of course, didn't have a griddle iron in the middle of it). That was enough for the buggane. He was off, for if Finn was that strong and the baby that big, he wasn't going to stick around for a fight.

Finn was stiff after being scrunched up in the cradle for so long, and he was glad to stop looking like a fool and get back into his own clothes, but he was very proud of his clever wife, who had sent the fearsome buggane running away in terror without Finn himself having to lift a finger in battle.

❧

This story appears in *Manx Fairy Tales* by Sophia Morrison (1911), and in *The Green Glass Bottle – Folk Tales from the Isle of Man* by Zena Carus (1975). I believe an Irish version of the story also exists where Finn is in Ireland, and his wife plays the same trick on a neighbouring giant who comes looking for a fight.

THE LAZY WIFE

Well, there was a woman once, and she was *incredibly* lazy. She was *so* lazy that she would do nothing but sit in the corner of the cottage warming herself beside the fire, or go around the other houses in the village gossiping all day. She did love a good gossip. Now this woman had a husband, a good man, and a patient one – he had to be, married to her – but even his patience ran out one day. He was tired of always wearing ragged, worn-out clothes, for his wife never patched or mended his things, and she certainly never made him anything new to wear. He had asked her to repair his old rags until he was blue in the face, but all he could get out of her was 'Traa dy liooar' ('Time enough')! So one day this husband gives his wife some wool to spin for him, so that he could have some new clothes.

He placed some sacks of wool on the floor in front of her, saying, 'Here is some wool for you to spin, and if it's not done by this time next month I'll turn you out of the house, and you can fend for yourself. You and your "Time enough!" have left me threadbare, and I won't stand for it anymore!' He thought that if he gave her a deadline, and a good reason to get to work, she'd set to and get the job done. He really should have known better.

His wife was far too lazy to spin, but she pretended to be working hard whenever the husband was in the house. She used to put the wheel down on the floor of the cottage every night before the husband came in from work, to make him think that she had been spinning, and scatter a few handfuls of fleece about the place.

The husband started to ask her if the thread was almost spun, because the spinning wheel seemed to be out so often that the thread *must* be almost ready to take to the weavers. He wasn't expecting his wife to weave the cloth herself – he knew that that skill was beyond her – but anyone could spin, or so he thought, since every woman and girl in the village seemed to be constantly at their wheels. After three week though, his wife had only spun one ball of wool, and that was lumpy and knotted and coarse as gorse. She knew the weaver wouldn't want to turn it into cloth, and her husband couldn't wear it if he did. That was part of the problem, you see. Because she was lazy when she was younger, she'd never bothered to learn to spin well … and because she couldn't do it properly, she put off doing it at all. What was the point, when it was all going to come out wrong anyway? But she didn't want to admit to her husband that this was something she couldn't do … so she did what a lot of us would do in that situation. She carried on pretending and hoped the problem would somehow solve itself. They very rarely do, however.

So after three weeks, when her husband asked her how many balls of wool she'd spun, and if there was enough ready to take to the weaver in a few days time, the woman was in a quandary. She couldn't say that just one ball was ready, in case her husband really did throw her out, so instead she said, 'I don't know, maybe we should count the balls.'

Now you might be thinking to yourself that this was a foolish thing for her to suggest. After all, it would only take a moment for her husband to count one single ball. But this woman was lazy, not stupid … she'd guessed that this was coming and she'd come up with a plan!

She'd put the sacks of wool up on the floor above. This area wasn't like the upstairs in a modern house … there were no stairs, for a start, and the flooring up there was only at one end of the cottage. If they had had children, the little ones would have slept up there, but children were another thing the woman had never quite got round to. Up the ladder she went to this little area under the roof, and then the game began. She ran and fetched her ball of wool, and threw it down to her husband.

'You keep count of the balls yourself, and fling them back up to me. I don't want them all down there, cluttering up the place.'

And as fast as he flung the ball up to her, so fast she flung it down to him again. When he had counted the same ball about twenty times, she said, 'That's the lot'. The husband was amazed … and impressed. He'd never really expected her to do that well.

'You've done a good job, my love, and spun a fair few balls of wool, more than enough to take to the weaver next week. I'm very proud of you,' said her husband, giving her a big kiss, and an even bigger hug.

Her pride in tricking him melted to dust and ashes … this was her husband, who loved her, and she loved him in return, even if her love was of the casual, 'not putting yourself out too much' variety. Now she was in a terrible fix … the truth was bound to come out, and when it did her husband, kind man that he was, would be disappointed in her. At the thought of that, she felt her heart begin to tighten. Even if he didn't throw her out, and she was fairly sure he wouldn't, not really, he would feel that she had let him down, and despite the fact that she had been letting him down for years, suddenly she couldn't bear the thought of it. But what could she do? She'd been lying to him for weeks now; she didn't dare turn round and tell him the truth. All that night she tossed and turned … for the first time in many years she'd discovered that she had a conscience, and it was pricking her, and keeping her awake.

Morning came, and with it an idea. It wasn't a terribly good one, but 'beggars can't be choosers', so she really couldn't do anything else. She had heard that there was a giant, living up on the mountain, who was good at all kinds of work, and especially spinning. She didn't know what the creature would demand in return for his help, but her husband gave her another proud smile as he set off for work, and that settled the matter. She couldn't face being the one to wipe that loving look off his face.

As soon as her man was gone, she fetched the wheelbarrow, and loaded the sacks of wool into it. Then she wheeled it up hills and down valleys until, at last, she came to the giant's house. She was pretty tired when she arrived, I can tell you, though it never occurred to her that she'd just done a good day's work getting the wool there. All she could think of was covering up her lies, and keeping the smile on her husband's face.

Once she was there, however, she had another thought … what would the giant do to her?

'What do you want?' demanded the giant, seeing the woman standing nervously in his doorway.

'I want your help,' she said, and went on to tell him the whole story. Strange how it's sometimes easier to tell one's troubles to a stranger, even a big, scary one, rather than to someone closer to home.

The giant thought for a few minutes, and then he nodded, saying, 'I'll spin the wool for you … if you can tell me my name when you come to collect the balls of wool a week from today. Are you satisfied?'

'Why shouldn't I be satisfied?' replied the woman; for she thought to herself it would be a very strange thing indeed if she couldn't find out his name within a week, especially as she was so good at gossiping. She was bound to be able to wheedle the information out of someone. She was so confident that she didn't even bother to ask the giant what would happen if she failed.

Well, over the next few days the woman tried every way she could think of to discover the giant's name, but, wherever she went and whoever she asked, she couldn't find out the truth, for no one had ever heard tell of it. Time was running out fast, and she was no nearer learning his name. Now there was just one more day left before she was due to return to the giant and give him her answer in exchange for the spun wool.

She had had a few sleepless nights by now, wishing she's asked the giant what might happen if she couldn't guess correctly. Perhaps he would just keep the wool that he'd spun, but then her husband would find out the truth and he'd be angry and disappointed, and the wool would all be gone. No new clothes for him. That would be bad enough, but what if the giant wanted more? What if he wanted to eat her? She wasn't entirely sure what giants ate, but after a number of restless nights it was easy enough to imagine the worst.

Now, as it happened, her husband was coming home over the mountain that day, early in the evening, and as he neared the giant's house, he saw that it was blazing with light. He heard noisy whirling and whistling, and as he got nearer his ears rang with singing, and laughing, and shouting. So he crept towards the window and peeped in, and there was the giant sitting at a wheel, spinning like the wind, and his hands were flying back and forth with the thread. The huge creature was shouting at the whistling wheel, calling out, 'Spin, wheel, spin faster; sing, wheel, sing louder!'

And he as he sang the wheel whirled faster and faster, in time with his song:

Snieu, queeyl, snieu; 'rane, queeyl, 'rane;
Dy chooilley clea er y thie, snieu er my skyn.
Lheeish yn ollan, lhiams y snaie,
S'beg fys t'ec yn ven litcheragh,
Dy re Mollyndroat my ennym!

Spin, wheel, spin; sing, wheel, sing;
Every beam on the house, spin overhead.
Herself's is the wool, mine is the thread,
How little she knows, the lazy wife,
That my name is Mollyndroat!

When the husband got home late that evening, his wife didn't scold him, even though she'd cooked him a fine dinner and it had gone cold. She thought it might be her last chance to please him, so she'd done her best for him. Her best wasn't wonderful, it has to be said, but it was better than her usual cooking. Trying to heat up the meal without burning it, she asked, 'What made you so late, tonight, my dear? Did something exciting happen? Have you heard anything new? You know how I like to keep up with the gossip!'

'Indeed I do,' replied her husband, 'and for once I've some for you.' He gave her a big grin, as they sat down to share their meal, and talk about the events of the day.

'For the last time,' thought the wife, sadly.

Her husband munched slowly on a potato, trying to find a bit that wasn't burnt. 'You know,' he muttered, 'I reckon *you* are a pretty fine spinner, my dear, but tonight I saw someone much better than you. Never in all my born days did I see such spinning, and hear such singing as I overheard at the giant's house tonight. That man can spin wool finer than a spider's web, for all that his hands look so big and clumsy.'

'What was he singing?' asked the wife, trying not to sound too desperate. 'Can you sing the giant's song for me, my dear? I should love to hear it.' Her husband blushed, saying that he wasn't much of a singer, not like the giant, but he'd do his best to sing her the song, and he did:

Snieu, queeyl, snieu; 'rane, queeyl, 'rane;
Dy chooilley clea er y thie, snieu er my skyn.
Lheeish yn ollan, lhiams y snaie,
S'beg fys t'ec yn ven litcheragh,
Dy re Mollyndroat my ennym!

Spin, wheel, spin; sing, wheel, sing;
Every beam on the house, spin overhead.
Herself's is the wool, mine is the thread,
How little she knows, the lazy wife,
That my name is Mollyndroat!

Well, the woman could have danced for joy when she heard the song, and got her husband to sing it again, and again, until she knew it off by heart. She gave her husband a big, grateful hug, though the poor man didn't know why she was so pleased with him … still, it was rather nice, having his wife treating him so well. He wasn't to know that she thought he had just saved her life, though he would have been glad enough to help, if he had known what was going on, for he truly loved his wife, for all her faults.

That night the woman slept soundly for the first time in over a week. As soon as her husband had gone out for the day, she took the empty wheelbarrow and pushed it to the giant's house, smiling and singing to herself as she went, to cheer herself up, as the journey was long and rather lonely. The song she chose to sing was her own version of the giant's song, and it raised her spirits as she walked:

Snieu, queeyl, snieu; snieu, queeyl, snieu;
Dy chooilley vangan er y villey, snieu er my skyn.
S'lesh hene yn ollan, as lhiam pene y snaie,
Son shenn Mollyndroat cha vow eh dy braa.

Spin, wheel, spin; spin, wheel, spin;
Every branch on the tree, spin overhead.
The wool is Himself's, the thread is my own,
For old Mollyndroat will never get it.

When she got to the house, she found the door open and in she went, walking bravely up to the giant.

'I've come back for the thread,' she said, trying to sound confident ... which was a little harder face to face with the giant, rather than in her imagination. He definitely seemed bigger than he had the week before, but the pile of beautifully spun wool was bigger too, wool that would make her husband proud of her, wool that would provide her man with new clothes ... wool that she was determined to take home with her.

'Hold on there, my good woman' said the giant. 'If you don't tell me my name, you're not getting the thread. That was the bargain, and you've only got three guesses. Now, what's my name?' The giant grinned, convinced that the woman would never guess it.

He looked so smug that the woman decided to have a bit of a game with him, so she said, 'Lots of names on the Island begin with Molly ... would your name be one of those?' The giant nodded, surprised, but he wasn't too worried. After all, lots of Manx names *started* with Molly, it was how they *ended* that mattered in this case, and she'd never guess that, for his name was uncommon, and she only had two guesses left.

'Is it Mollychreest?' she asked, playfully, as if she didn't know where to start guessing. The giant disliked being teased, and wanted to get the whole thing over with, so that he could keep the thread he had spun. He even considered keeping the woman too, though he didn't usually eat people these days. It tended to annoy the neighbours, and bring mobs with flaming torches up into the mountains to attack him. Just the wool then, he thought, regretfully. There were many names beginning with Molly for her to try, and she only had one guess left. Suddenly the woman stopped laughing and smiling, pointed a finger at him and said, with deadly seriousness:

S'lesh hene yn ollan, as lhiam pene y snaie,
Son shenn-Moll-YN-DROAT cha vow eh dy braa.

The wool is Himself's, and the thread is my own,
For old-Moll-YN-DROAT will never get it.

Well, the giant, he had lost, and he knew it. It put him in a terrible rage and he shouted at her, 'Bad luck to you! You could never have found out my name unless you're a wicked fortune teller.'

'Bad luck to you yourself, you great lump,' she shouted back at him, 'for trying to steal a decent woman's wool.'

'Oh, go to the Devil, you and your evil fortune-telling ways,' he raged and in his anger, he began to pelt her with the balls of wool. The woman was a good catch, and each ball flung at her was caught, and tossed into the wheelbarrow. When every last ball of yarn was back in her possession, she turned on her heel and pushed the wheelbarrow home.

When her husband came back from work that day, there was the barrow, full of the finest spun wool you could possibly imagine ... and if he noticed it was rather better spun than the lumpy balls he'd counted the week before ... well, he was wise enough, and kind enough, not to mention it. He took the wool to the weaver, and got so much cloth back that he was able get a new dress made for his wife, as well as the clothes he needed.

As for his lazy wife, she had discovered that she rather liked making her husband proud and happy, and if that meant a *little* extra work, well, perhaps it was worth it. She had to learn to spin in secret, of course, and even when she got good at it, her spinning didn't compare to the giant's handiwork. Her husband never noticed though – or at least he never said anything – and so they muddled along much better after that ... not that it's any of our business!

⁂

Herself is often a reference to a wife, and Himself is a reference to a husband.

One of the reasons I like this tale is that it shows some of the cultural roots of the Island. Some people reading it would think it's a version of 'Rumplestiltskin', first collected by the Brothers Grimm in Germany, and so had come to the Island from Europe. In fact, it's much closer to the story of 'Gilitrutt', from Iceland, which involves an ogress (ogres and trolls being important in Icelandic stories) rather than a giant, but is otherwise almost identical. This would suggest that the story was actually brought to the Island by the Vikings.

In the original version of the tale, the wife has more guesses, and runs through a number of names – Mollyrea, Mollyruiy, Mollyvridey, Mollychreest, Mollyvoirrey, Mollyvartin and Mollycharaine – before coming out with Moll-YN-DROAT. I found in the telling of this tale that limiting it to three guesses worked better for audiences, so that's the way I choose to tell it, but somebody else might decide to use all the names.

This tale is in *Manx Fairy Tales* by Sophia Morrison (1911).

THE OLD MAN

Now you've already heard that Castle Rushen was said to be famous for its underground passages, and there were those who believed that these led to a beautiful country underground, inhabited by giants. Many people tried to explore these tunnels, but almost all of them failed.

Once, however, a group of men were sitting in an inn, drinking together, and their conversation turned to the underground tunnels, and to giants. They all knew that some men had made their way into the tunnels and never been seen again … others had come out saying they couldn't find their way at all, and vowing never to go back down. The men in this tale, sitting in the inn, nursing their ale before a roaring fire, had an idea. Often such ideas, fuelled by drink and good company, are not such good ones in the cold light of day. This idea, however, *was* a good one … to go down into the tunnels below Castle Rushen in a group, rather than alone. There is safety in numbers, after all.

They arranged to explore the tunnels the following night, and each agreed to bring something that might be useful for the expedition. One fellow brought torches, and a tinderbox to light them, so that they could see their way. Another brought ropes,

in case anyone fell down a hole and needed rescuing. The third man brought a length of iron, to use as a crowbar, in case they found any treasure chests … they were an optimistic bunch. The fourth man brought a piece of chalk, to mark their route, so that they could find their way back.

By the light of the flaming torches they entered the tunnels beneath the castle, and began to wander along them, marking their path with the chalk. They walked for what seemed like hours, sometimes in level passageways, but mostly downhill. Suddenly they rounded a bend and came across an old man of great size. 'It's a giant!' whispered one of the explorers, unnecessarily. Indeed it was, and the enormous fellow had a long beard, and pale sightless eyes. He was sitting on a rock, looking as if he had always been there, and would always be there, and the men were nervous about disturbing him. Perhaps he was some kind of guard, protecting the entrance to the land of the giants.

The giant heard them approach, however, and turned his head towards them, asking how things fared on the Island. After a short conversation, for in truth the men were too scared to say much, the giant asked if one of them would be willing to shake his hand, as a sign of goodwill. Looking at the giant's massive fist, all of them were reluctant to put their puny hands in his. Finally, after much nudging and shoving, the man with the iron crowbar stepped forward and held it out to the giant, who squeezed it so hard that it bent out of shape. 'It is good to know,' said the old giant, smiling, 'that there are yet men in the Isle of Man. Men strong enough to protect the Island, as we once did.'

The old giant settled back into a drowsy sleep, and the group of friends, deciding that they had had enough of an adventure for one night, followed their chalk marks back to the entrance of the tunnels, and made their way to the pub.

One of them suggested that they should repeat the experience another time. Perhaps a second attempt would enable them to find the underground country itself ... or even a giant's abandoned treasure. He tried to fix a date and time with his fellows, but somehow they were all a little busy. One had sheep that were about to lamb, another felt he should spend more time at home with his wife, and so on. In the end, they never did go back down into the tunnels ... most of them felt that one close encounter with a giant was quite enough. No need to go looking for more trouble.

✍

This legend is found in *The Folklore of the Isle of Man* by A.W. Moore (1891).

THE SPELLBOUND GIANT

Castle Rushen lies in the south-eastern part of the Island, in Castletown. The castle itself is one of the best-preserved medieval castles in Europe, and well worth a visit. It was originally built for a Norse king in 1265 and developed by various rulers up until the sixteenth century. It has been used as a fortress, a royal home, a mint, and a prison, and today you can wander through the kitchens, the gatehouse, the great hall and various other rooms,

✍

and even up on to the roof. But you *can't* go exploring underneath the castle, oh no. That would be a very bad idea because if you did … you might never come back.

The legend says that there is a room in Castle Rushen that has never been opened within the memory of man, because there is 'something of enchantment' in it. It is said that the castle was at first inhabited by fairies, and afterwards by giants, who continued to live there until the time of Merlin, the magician who, by force of magic, drove most of them away, and bound the rest in spells, which will last until the end of time.

This story is of one of those giants. There are supposed to be many beautiful underground rooms beneath the castle, far finer than any of those above. In the past a number of brave men ventured down to explore the secrets of this subterraneous palace, but none of them ever returned to speak of what they saw; it was, therefore, decided that all entrances to it should be kept permanently shut, so that no one else should be lost.

Now some time in 1670, a man who had a great reputation for being brave, asked the guardians of these entrances for permission to go down into the caverns and see if the legends were true. He was, of course, told 'No', so he asked again, and again, and kept on asking until at last they agreed, if only to shut him up.

Now this man was not only brave, but wise. He was a man who prepared, and he took down into the tunnels with him a ball of twine, or packthread. He tied one end of this near the entrance, and unravelled the ball as he went exploring, so that he would be able to find his way back to where he started.

He went through a number of underground chambers, each of them further beneath the earth than the last. After walking through these for about a mile, he began to see a little gleam of light, which seemed to come from far away, but filled him with longing to reach it.

As he approached the brightening light he saw that it came from a very large and magnificent house, lit from within by candles. This was the light that had drawn him forward. The house itself seemed to fill the whole passageway, leaving no route around it.

He knocked three times at the front door, which was eventually answered by a servant, who asked the man what he wanted. 'I want to travel on as far as I can,' replied the brave adventurer, 'but I can't see any path to take, except back the way that I have come.'

The servant explained that the only way forward was to go through the house itself, then he led the brave man along various hallways, and let him out of the back door. The explorer continued walking though the dark tunnels for some considerable distance, and then, up ahead, he saw another house, even more magnificent than the first, and again the windows blazed with candlelight. He was about to knock at the front door of *this* house when something caught his eye. Glancing in through a window beside the door, he found himself looking down into a parlour, the floor of which seemed to be built at a lower level than the rest of the house, although the ceiling was quite high. This held an enormous black marble table, running the entire length of the room, and on the table – stretched along its full length – he saw a man, though it seemed to him to be more like a monster; fourteen feet long, and ten or eleven foot around the body. This incredible creature lay as if it was sleeping, with his massive head on a book, and a huge sword beside him. The man, his hand raised to knock on the door, paused. Did he really want to risk waking this frightful giant? What if there were more giants inside? What if they ate uninvited travellers for breakfast?

He decided to turn back … I did say that he was wise as well as brave, didn't I? Following the thread, he made his way to the first house and hammered on the back door. The same servant opened it, and guided him to the front of the house, putting the man on the right path. The adventurer turned to the servant and asked, 'What would have happened if I had carried on, if I'd knocked at the door of the second house?'

The servant paused, and then replied, 'You would have found others to keep you company … but you would never have been able to return. Just as well that you had not only the courage to make the journey, but the wisdom to know when to stop, too.'

The man tried to ask more about the houses, and the sleeping giant, but the servant said that humans were not supposed to know of such things, and refused to answer any more questions.

So the explorer said farewell, turned away from the servant, and began his return journey. Using the twine as a guide, and running his fingers along it, he retraced his steps, up and up, until at last he reached the world he'd left behind him, and found himself in the safety of Castle Rushen. He told his tale to the guardians of the entrances into the underground chambers, and everyone agreed that it would be safest for these doorways to be sealed up, permanently, so that no one could go exploring again ... and any giant, on waking, would find it difficult to come up inside the castle. Every entrance to the chambers below was closed and barred that very night ... and they have remained so to this day. Which means, of course, that the giant might still be down there, sleeping!

❦

This very old tale was told to George Waldron, a collector of Manx tales, who lived and worked on the Island from 1720 to 1730, it also appears in *The Folklore of the Isle of Man* by A.W. Moore (1891), and in *The Folklore of the Isle of Man* by Margaret Killipp (1975).

6

THE MYSTERIES
OF THE SEA

BEWARE THE BEN-VARREY

Long ago, when fishing boats were small, and families were large, five brothers were out at sea in the family boat, fishing. The catch was good and they were all working hard when one of them, the youngest and the handsomest, stopped what he was doing, lifted his head and stared out to sea.

When his brothers asked him what was wrong he said, 'Listen, can't you hear it? It's the most beautiful singing I ever heard.' His brothers were puzzled, for none of them could hear anything, but the youngest brother kept staring longingly out into the distance, looking for the singer. Now that he had heard her voice, he wanted to see her for himself.

The other brothers realised that he must be hearing a ben-varrey, which means a woman of the sea, a mermaid, and that she was trying to charm their little brother into joining her in the water. They made as much noise as they could, singing and humming and shouting, to block out the sound, as they steered the boat back to the harbour. However, their brother remained in a drowsy trance for days afterwards. For months the brothers chose to fish in other waters, and avoided the part of the sea where the ben-varrey had been heard. Eventually, they began to forget that the strange event had ever happened.

The following spring the youngest brother took his own little boat out to the area where the ben-varrey had sung, because another fisherman had told him that catches were particularly good there just then and he wanted to see for himself. If there were plenty of fish in the area, he would suggest to his brothers that it was time they brought the bigger family boat into that area again. Nobody else had reported hearing the song of the ben-varrey in all the months that had passed since he was last there. It must be safe to return by now, he thought. But it wasn't! The ben-varrey had been silent because she was waiting for him, and him alone.

As soon as the young fisherman neared the rock that she was lying on, the ben-varrey started to sing, and the man fell under her spell once more. Without his brothers there to distract him and get him safely back to land, the fisherman found himself drawn nearer and nearer the rocks, charmed by her lovely voice. When he saw her face he was lost, for she was the most beautiful and the kindest-looking creature he had ever seen. Her hair was long and green, as was her fishlike tail, and her skin was the softest pink. She slid off the rocks and into the water, calling out, 'Follow me, my dearest, follow me.' And follow her he did, rowing with all his might to keep up. Whenever he grew tired and thought about turning back, she sang

again, drawing him to her, and he had to carry on. At last he could see an island in the distance. He knew it wasn't the Isle of Man for that was far behind him. This was an island he had never seen before. He was sure it wasn't on any chart or map.

When he reached the island he pulled his little boat up on to the sand, and the ben-varrey told him to pick her up and carry her into a great cave, where all the mer-people were dancing and singing in a deep pool of water. He was entranced by the beauty and the strangeness of it all. As well as the mermaids and mermen, he could see other shapes, ghostlike wraiths, misty and shivering in the corners. The ben-varrey in his arms began to sing again, and he forgot about everyone else as he gazed longingly into her eyes. She told him to set her down on a nearby rock and sit beside her. Then she reached out and picked up a goblet off the rocks, and held it out to him saying, 'Here, drink some of this my dear, you must be thirsty after your long journey.' The young fisherman suddenly realised that he was thirsty, desperately thirsty, and took the goblet from her.

He was just about to take a sip of the amber liquid it was filled with, when he noticed the ghostly figures again. Three of them, all dressed as fishermen, were signalling to him. Their tattered clothing was as insubstantial as the men themselves, their hair was wild and tangled, but their eyes were piercing bright. The first placed his hands over his eyes, as if to say, 'Don't look at her', the second moved his hands over his ears, meaning 'Don't listen to her', and the third had covered his mouth with his hand, to tell the fisherman not to drink from the cup. It reminded the young man of an ornament on his mother's mantelpiece at home. It was of three monkeys with their hands in just those positions, meaning 'See No Evil. Hear No Evil. Speak No Evil'. Surely this beautiful mermaid couldn't be evil? But the memory of home – the first thought of home he had had since he heard the ben-varrey's voice out at sea – made him hesitate before drinking from the goblet.

Seeing him pause, she turned and saw the ghostly figures, all trying to warn him not to drink anything, for they knew he would be trapped there forever if he did … just as they had been when they were young and handsome … and alive. The ben-varrey's face twisted with rage. No longer was she beautiful and kind looking, but hideous and menacing. She looked as if she would have killed the ghosts on the spot, if they weren't already dead. Seeing such a change in her broke the spell she had over the young fisherman, and flinging the goblet to the ground he rushed outside to his boat. He didn't want to be trapped here with such a creature forever. But his boat had been smashed into tiny pieces while he was in the cave. It would never carry him to sea again.

He leapt into the water, determined to swim all the way home. It was a long and difficult journey, even though he was a strong swimmer, but finally he washed up on the shore. Home at last, and glad to be so. He stumbled along towards the house, where he lived with his mother and brothers, but as he passed a shop window he saw his own reflection. His clothes were in rags, and his hair had grown long and matted, streaked with grey. He had a straggly, greying beard too. How long had he been gone?

When he reached the house he found the answer. Sixteen years had passed since he set out in his little boat, though it felt like only a few days to him. His mother had died many years before, and all his brothers were married, with families of their own. His oldest brother now lived in the family home, and much had changed about it, but his mother's favourite monkey ornament still stood on the mantelpiece ... 'See No Evil. Hear No Evil. Speak No Evil'.

Now the fisherman felt that he didn't belong anywhere. Home wasn't really his home anymore – too many things had changed. Although the ben-varrey had frightened him, he still longed to hear her beautiful voice again. He spent the rest of his days down by the shore, looking to see if the magical island would reappear on the horizon and listening for the song of the ben-varrey ... but now he wasn't the youngest, and now he wasn't the handsomest, and the ben-varrey never came back.

Other versions of this story appear in *The Green Glass Bottle – Folk Tales from the Isle of Man* by Zena Carus (1975) and in *Tales from The Celtic Countries* by Rhiannon Ifans (1999).

THE WITCH OF SLIEU WHALLIAN

About two miles from Peel, opposite to the Tynwald Mount, there is a hill called Slieu Whallian, said to be haunted by the spirit of a murdered witch. She never appears to mortal eyes, but every night she weeps and wails, adding her cries to the howling of the wind.

When she was alive she had understood the wind. Some people even believed that she could control it, for she was one of the wise women that sold fair winds. You might wonder how anyone could sell the wind … but these women could, bound up in the knots in a length of thread. The sailors would buy these 'fair winds' off a wise woman and take them to sea with them. When the weather was calm, and wind was needed for the sails, the sailors were to loosen two of the knots … but the third knot was never to be undone, or a hurricane would be unleashed and the sailors would be shipwrecked.

In those days, sailors were a superstitious lot, holding tightly to their traditions. Nobody was to whistle on board, because whistling 'bothered the wind'. Even in a dead calm, whistling up the wind was never to be tried, the *correct* charm for raising the wind was to stick a knife into the mast, on the side from which it was hoped that the wind would then blow, or of course, to buy 'fair winds' from a wise woman.

Even which words they used on board mattered to the sailors back then, and many things had both sea-names and land-names. No four-footed creature was mentioned at sea by its land-name, so a hare would be the 'fellow with the long ears', a cat was a 'scraper', and a rat 'a long-tailed fellow'. Even today most people on the Isle of Man don't use the R.A.T. word, but always call them 'long-tails'. Custom and tradition were very important then, giving people a sense of security, and a way to understand and control the world, and especially the forces of nature.

Well, this story starts on Midsummer Day in Peel, and the herring fleet was ready to go to sea. The men had finished their tasks on land, the barley was sown, the potatoes were in the ground … all was prepared so that there would be food to harvest on the land in the autumn. Now it was time to harvest the sea.

The fishing boats were rigged, the nets were stowed on board ready, there was just one more tradition to complete before the fleet could sail. The wise woman who sold the 'fair winds' was standing beside the harbour with the rest of the women and children, waiting to watch the fleet sail.

A bowl of water was brought from the holy well and given to her to look into, so that she could predict the luck of the fleet, as she did every year. Everyone was joking and smiling, hoping she'd announce a bumper catch of herring, or at least a good one. It was a fine day and the sky was clear, with just a fair amount of wind coming from the north. Conditions were perfect ... surely the woman would predict 'the best catch ever'. She didn't. As soon as she looked into the bowl of water she grew pale, and gasped in horror, 'Do you know what I'm seeing?'

'Tell us,' said people in the crowd, alarmed at her expression.

'I'm seeing the wild waves lashed to foam away by great Bradda Head,
'I'm seeing the surge round the Chicken's Rock and the breaker's lip is red;
'I'm seeing where corpses toss in the Sound, with nets and gear and spars,
'And never a one of the fishing fleet is riding under the stars.'

'A storm?' muttered one of the wives in the silence that followed the wise woman's words.

'She's predicting a storm,' added another.

'With not a boat left afloat,' said a third.

The wise woman nodded, hoping the fishermen would believe her prediction and not put out to sea. Then they would be safe.

The men, meanwhile, were huddled together talking amongst themselves, until the admiral of the fishing fleet, a man named Gorry, marched over to the wise woman, snatched the basin out of her hands and flung it into the sea. He shouted at her in his fury, 'I've a good mind to heave you into the sea after it, you witch, as sure as I'm alive! If I had my way all your sort would be run into the sea.' The woman looked at him in horror. Until that moment she had been a wise woman, someone people turned to for help and advice, part of the community. Now, because she had tried to warn them about the storm that was coming, she was being called a witch. She noticed some of the women take a step or two away from her, and knew that the admiral's comments would stick, she would be seen as a wise woman no more … from now on everyone would think of her as a witch. It would be worth it though, if that meant that they listened to her prediction, that they didn't put out to sea.

The admiral, however, wasn't about to let that happen. He jumped up on to a crate, to get the men's attention, and said, 'Boys, we're not going to lose a shot at a good catch just because of this witch, are we? You lad, Cashen, you need this catch to set you up for your wedding don't you?'

The young man nodded, bashfully, adding, 'Aye, no herring, no wedding.'

'Well then,' said the admiral, 'the weather is perfect, we can all see that. Don't let the witch's spite deprive us of a good catch. Let's go and chance it, with the help of God.' The men agreed and the fleet put to sea, though some of the wives tried quietly to convince their husbands not to go. The fishermen would not be persuaded, however, and every boat set sail with a full crew.

They sailed south and a fine breeze carried them to the fishing ground, where every man was on the lookout for all the telltale signs of herring. When the sun set all the boats shot their nets over the sides and into the sea. That was when the witch's prediction began to come true. The wind changed, a sudden gale blew up, and waves tossed the boats in all directions. The men hoisted the sails, trying to get home, but their anchors were dragging, the nets weighed them down, and the only light they had to see by was the lightning. The boats were smashed to pieces on the rocks of the Calf, and only two men survived.

There was one boat that escaped, however, and that was the boat of the *Seven Boys*. She was a boat from Dalby, and belonged to seven young men, who were all unmarried. Now these fishermen had always been good to the dooinney marrey, the merman, and when they were hauling in their nets they would throw him a dishful of herring. In return, they always seemed to have good luck with their fishing.

Well, after all the boats had shot their nets, and before the weather changed for the worse, the crew of this boat heard the merman calling out to them.

'It's calm and fine now, but soon there will be a storm coming.'

The skipper for that boat called his thanks to the merman, then turned to his crew and said, 'Every herring must hang by his own gills.' They all agreed that they should make their own decision as a crew, despite what the fleet had chosen to do. Ignoring *two* warnings would be foolish, so even though the night was still fair, they hauled in their nets and sailed back to the harbour.

As for the wise woman … sorry, the witch … you'd think everyone would be grateful to her for trying to warn the fishermen, but you'd think wrong. *She* was blamed for everything – the storms, the deaths, the loss of the fleet. It was a terrible disaster for the town, for so many men were lost, so many families left without husbands and fathers. Everyone was in a dreadful state, but that doesn't really excuse what they did.

People said that the witch had used her magic to raise the storm. They dragged her up to the top of the mountain, Slieu Whallian, and put her into a barrel studded with sharp iron spikes, pointing inwards. They hammered the lid on, to seal the barrel, and they rolled it from the top of the hill to the bottom, where it sank into the soft ground. For many years after that there was a bare track down the mountainside called 'The Witch's Way', where nothing would ever grow.

And so the murdered witch still haunts the mountain, never appearing to mortal eyes, but every night she weeps and wails, adding her cries to the howling of the wind, for when she was alive, she had understood the wind and perhaps howling with it brings her comfort.

ॐ

This story is mentioned in *The Folklore of the Isle of Man* by A.W. Moore (1891) and in *Manx Fairy Tales* by Sophia Morrison (1911), while some of the information about 'fair winds' and sea-names is in *The Folklore of the Isle of Man* by Margaret Killip (1975).

LUCK AND LAND EGGS

Now some of the ben-varrey, the women of the sea, could be dangerous, but not all mermaids behave in the same way. Long ago there
was a family, who went by the name of Sayle, and they lived beside a
little stream that ran down to the rocky shore. They always had good
fortune, or so it seemed to their neighbours, and never went short
of anything. To be fair, they were a hard-working bunch, always
turning their hand to whatever task needed doing. They made their
living by fishing, but the men also wove lobster pots, for there were
plenty of rushes growing nearby, and their work was good, so the
pots sold well. The women looked after the cow, some chickens
and a small flock of sheep, as well as growing their own vegetables.
Everything they had was shared evenly around the family, with one
exception. They had a little apple tree, and the head of the household always had the pick of the crop. He seemed terribly fond of
apples, which earned him the nickname 'Pip', and whenever he put
out to sea in their little boat, he always took several apples with him.
All the years that Pip Sayle was fishing for a living, everything went
well for the family. Their boat was safe at sea, even in bad weather,
their crops grew well, and they all stayed healthy.

However, old age comes to us all in the end, and eventually Pip had
to leave most of the boat work to his sons, and from that point on
the family's luck diminished. Catches were smaller, crops didn't grow
as well and often they only had food on the table if one of the boys
went hunting in the hills. Most of Pip's sons scattered, some going
off with the herring fleet, and some looking for other ways to earn
a living. The youngest of them, however, stayed at home to help his
parents and keep things going. His name was Evan, and he split his
time between working the land, and taking the little fishing boat out.

One day Evan was out in the boat, and when he'd caught
enough fish, he decided to pull the boat up on to the beach and go
looking for wild bird's eggs to add to their meal, for their chickens
had stopped laying … another piece of bad luck. When he had
finished his task, and was returning to the beach with several eggs
in his pockets, he heard a voice calling out to him.

He turned and saw a fine-looking woman sitting on the edge of a rock. She waved at him and beckoned him over. As he headed in her direction, he noticed her legs … or rather the lack of them. He had assumed that the woman's legs would be dangling in the water, but on closer inspection he realised that it was a big fishy tail that curved over the rock and into the sea. He was a little frightened, for mermaids have a dangerous reputation, but her smile was kind, so he moved slightly closer.

'How's your father?' the mermaid asked. 'I haven't seen him in a long time.' Trying hard to look as if talking to a mermaid was a perfectly normal thing to do, Evan explained that his father was now too old and frail to go out in the boat, and that the rest of his brothers had moved away. 'Well, I hope that you don't move away, young man, I'd like to see you again,' and with that, she slid into the water and disappeared.

When Evan got home he told his father about the strange creature he'd met on the shore, and his father's face lit up with joy. 'The family will be lucky again now,' declared Pip Sayle, adding, 'make sure you take some apples with you, the next time you go that way … then we'll see what happens.' A look of fond remembrance crossed the old man's face, as he recalled the pleasant times that he'd spent with the mermaid in his younger days.

The very next day the young man went out in the boat, taking some apples with him, and when he got to the place where he had seen the beautiful woman of the sea, he pulled the boat up on the beach again. Then, since there was no sign of her, he went hunting for eggs, up amongst the rocks. He was beginning to think that he'd imagined the whole encounter. His sleep had been destroyed by dreams of her … and in each dream he had her beauty seemed to increase. Surely such a lovely creature only existed in his imagination.

He was pushing his boat back into the water when he heard someone singing. Now the song of a ben-varrey can drive a man mad, but the mermaid chose not to use her voice in that way. Her singing was sweet, and warmed his heart, but did not compel him to turn to her. Turn he did though, with a smile on his face, delighted to see her again. There she was, bobbing in the water, leaning into the boat to reach for one of the apples, and smiling at him. She held up an apple and began to chant:

> The luck of the sea be with you, but don't forgetful be
> Of bringing some sweet land eggs, for the children of the sea.

Then she took a bite of the crisp green apple, and sank down under the waves. Now he knew why his father had always had first pick of the apples … he had taken them to keep the mermaid happy, and bring his family luck!

Every day after that, Evan went to meet with her, and take her a sweet 'land egg'. He spent so much time down on the shore that his mother began to scold him for idleness, and even his father suggested that he was spending a little too much time with the mermaid. The family began to prosper, however, so he didn't get into too much trouble. In return for all the apples, the mermaid didn't only give the family the luck of the sea. She also told Evan stories … tales of life under the water, and of strange exotic places visited by other creatures of the oceans.

With every meeting the mermaid grew fonder of the young man, while every tale she told him sparked his interest in travelling. The very method she was using to encourage him to visit her was giving him a taste for travel … and travel, of course, would take him away from her. Sure enough, one day as they sat together on the rocks in the sunshine, Evan announced his decision to go and explore the world, by taking a job on a trading ship. To his surprise the mermaid burst into tears, for she didn't want to part with him. The young man thought her distress was because now there would be no one to bring her an apple every day. He decided to cheer her up by planting an apple tree at the top of a nearby cliff. He explained to her that even when he was far away, this tree would grow land eggs which, when they were ripe and sweet and ready for eating, would drop into the sea of their own accord, so that she could eat them. He asked her to let the family keep its good luck, and even after Evan went away, things went well for them.

The mermaid waited patiently for the apples to ripen, sitting on the rocks in the evening, singing mournful songs and looking longingly up at the tree above. She'd never waited for fruit to grow before, and found it a long, slow business. At last she had to admit to herself that it wasn't only the apples she was missing, but Evan himself, who she'd come to value more than anything … even her favourite 'land eggs'. She concluded that she couldn't be happy unless she could be with the young man she had grown so fond of, so she decided to go in search of him. If he was on a sailing ship, surely a mermaid could find him? She imagined the joy of seeing him again, and of them coming back together to this quiet shore, to share the apples between them, for she was certain the fruit would be ripe by the time they returned.

So both of them set off on their adventures, but neither of them ever came back, alone or together. Perhaps she found her young man and they chose to make a life together in some other part of the world; perhaps she searched and searched but never tracked him down … the oceans of the world are very large indeed and a single ship is very small. We'll never know how their story ended, though it is to be hoped that the luck of the sea kept both of them safe on their journeys.

Back on the Island, only the apple tree remained, as a reminder of their time together. Every autumn it proudly produced its 'land eggs', but no mermaids came to eat them, and no fishermen either. The apples dropped into the sea each year, and floated away, un-tasted.

~

This story is told in *Manx Fairy Tales* by Sophia Morrison (1911), under the title 'The Mermaid of Gob-ny-Ooyl'.

GHOST CHILD

Most children are welcomed into the world as a long-awaited addition to a loving family. Some, however, are not, and this is the tale of such a child. There was a woman who lived in a lonely farmhouse, so lonely that there might not be any visitors to it for months at a time … although this woman must have entertained a visitor about nine months before our story starts.

The woman was due to inherit the farm off her father when his time came, and they all agreed that the land would make a fine dowry. It would allow the woman to attract a good husband, someone who would work the land and pass it on, in turn, down the family.

Well, whoever had visited the woman, nine months earlier, had not been interested in farming, or even with sticking around. He was long gone before the woman knew that she was expecting a child … and when the baby began to show, and her father guessed the truth, he was furious. How was she to attract a good husband now? The woman too was unhappy about the pregnancy. She was angry with the man for leaving, she was angry with herself for falling for his charms, and most of all, she was angry with the baby, for daring to exist at all.

The child was finally born into an unwelcoming world … and died almost as soon as the woman had given birth to it. Her father said that perhaps it was for the best, and the woman agreed. Nobody outside the family had seen the baby, or its mother, while she was pregnant. Her reputation could remain intact and she would still be able to marry a suitable man … unless, of course, they took the child to church for burial. Then the whole story would come out. So, instead, the mother carried the dead baby, in the dark of the night, along the narrow path over the rocks, past the Cave of the Goat to Lag ny Keeilley, which means 'the hollow of the chapel'. There, scattered across the ground, were the remains of a lonely little keeil, or chapel, that had stood on that spot for generations. She buried the child in the ruins, and left it there alone. She returned to the life that her family had planned for her, and they never spoke of the matter again.

Now some time after this, the fishing fleet was sailing up and down the coast out of Dalby, on the west side of the Island. They kept passing and re-passing Lag ny Keeilley, and they noticed something odd. They would see a beautiful light and hear weeping and wailing, in a voice that sounded like that of a little lost child.

The fishermen could see the light moving from the rocky coast up to the remains of the old keeil, and then it would go out. The men got so frightened that they didn't want to fish in those waters after dark. Instead, as soon as the sun began to set, they would sail back to Dalby and home.

This meant, of course, that they were catching less fish, which brought hardship to their families, and the women were worried for their men every time their husbands put to sea, in case the light had some ill purpose and the men never came home. Eventually people decided that something had to be done.

There was one old man, his name was Illiam Quirk, and because of his age he hadn't gone to sea for years, but he was a brave man, prepared to put his trust in God and the power of prayer. Well, he said he'd go out on one of the boats to see for himself what was happening, so off he went with the fishing fleet. They were near Lag ny Keeilley when the sun began to set, and the other boats sailed for home. Illiam Quirk told the crew of the boat that he was in to row nearer to the shore. The other men were terrified, but they trusted the old man, and did as he asked. It was a fine, beautiful moonlit night when he heard the crying start. Over and over again the little voice wailed, 'I am a little child without a name!'

'Pull nearer to the land,' said Illiam when he heard the child. They pulled close in, and he could see a little child on the shore holding a lighted candle in its hand.

'Then God bless me, you poor child, we must give you a name!' Illiam called out to the little figure. The old man took off his hat, stood up in the boat, and threw a handful of water towards the child, crying out: 'If you are a boy, I christen you Juan, in the name of the Father, Son, and Holy Ghost! If you are a girl I christen you Joanney, in the name of the Father, Son, and Holy Ghost!'

The ghostly figure gave a shy smile, and at once the crying stopped, the light went out, and the child with no name was never seen or heard again. Illiam turned to the crew of the boat and said, 'You'll be safe enough now, though the poor little thing wished you no harm ... it was just the spirit of a little unbaptised child, crying out to be freed from the world.'

The fishing fleet went back to working into the night, and the families went hungry no longer. As for Illiam Quirk, everyone was grateful to him for knowing what to do, and having the courage to do it, and the ghost of the little child was the most grateful of all.

෴

This tale occurs in *The Folklore of the Isle of Man* by A.W. Moore (1891) and *Manx Fairy Tales* by Sophia Morrison (1911), under the title 'The Child Without a Name', as well as in *The Green Glass Bottle – Folktales of the Isle of Man* by Zena Carus (1975).

෴

7

STRANGE AND REMARKABLE CREATURES

THE BUGGANE OF ST TRINIAN'S

Up near the Greeba Mountain there is a church without a roof. Some people call it St Trinian's, others refer to it as Keeill Brisht, the Broken Church. If you were to drive past it today, you'd think it was just an old church that had once served its community, but had now fallen into disrepair … but that's not the story at all. The church is said to have been built because of a promise made to God by a person who was caught up in a hurricane at sea hundreds of years ago.

The man was a merchant who had been born near there, and at that time the village didn't have a church. People had to walk a long way to go to church in the next village on a Sunday, which was difficult for the very old, or very young, and in bad weather some of the villagers couldn't get to church at all. The merchant promised God that if he survived the hurricane he would send money home to have a church built for the village. Well, the man did survive the storm and he kept his promise. He sent the money to the village and arranged for the church to be built, but the building was never finished. This was because the site the village chose for the church was directly over the lair of a mischievous buggane, who did not want church bells ringing out over his head every Sunday.

Now bugganes are hideous, evil, goblin-like spirits that can take any shape they choose. They live in the wild places of the Island, causing all sorts of trouble, and the buggane of St Trinian's was the most terrible one of all.

The buggane waited until the church was nearly finished, the walls were up and the roof almost complete, then he appeared in the church that night and forced up the roof beams, bringing the roof tumbling down, while letting out a terrible, fiendish laugh.

But the locals still wanted their church, so they put the roof on again. Once more the buggane waited until just one more day of work would complete the building, and then up through the floor he rose, pulling the roof down a second time, still laughing fiendishly.

Then someone suggested that perhaps, if a person was to stay in the church on the last night before the roof was finished, that would keep the buggane away … then the church could be completed the following morning, and the bishop could bless and consecrate it the moment it was ready, and the buggane would never be able to enter it, or damage it, again.

Everyone thought that this was a brilliant idea … but nobody wanted to be the person who stayed there overnight. Now Timothy, a local tailor, was a good man but a poor one. He wanted the village to have its church, but he also needed to earn some money, so he bet everyone that he could make a pair of breeches from scratch, in that one night, which would take some pretty fast work, and if he succeeded, he would earn himself a tidy sum. Now in those days there were no sewing machines … every stitch was done by hand, and nobody thought the tailor would be able to do that, in a church, in poor light, while waiting for the buggane to come, so plenty of people were prepared to place their bets.

For the third time the roof was built, and on the evening before the church was due to be finished, Timothy let himself into the building. He had fabrics and patterns, needles, pins and scissors, threads, a tape measure and tailor's chalk … everything he needed to make the breeches. He lit some candles so that he could see to work, seated himself on the floor in the chancel, and began to cut and tack and stitch as quickly as he could. He was so busy he almost forgot about the buggane, but just before dawn, when he had only a few stitches left to go before the breeches were finished, he looked up and thought, 'It worked, the buggane hasn't come.' He rethreaded his needle and returned to his sewing, but at that very moment the head of the frightful buggane began to rise up through the stone floor of the church in front of him and said, 'Do you see my great head, little man, my large eyes, my sharp teeth?' The buggane was truly terrible to look at, with horns on his head, a mane of coarse black hair and eyes like flaming torches.

'I see! I see!' replied the tailor, stitching with all his might, and without lifting his eyes from his work. To be honest, he was too terrified to look.

The buggane, still rising slowly out of the ground, hated being ignored and cried out even more loudly, 'Do you see my great body, little man, my large hands, my sharp nails?'

'I see! I see!' answered Timothy, still not looking, but continuing to stitch as fast as he could.

The buggane had now risen completely from the ground, the claws on his feet tapping angrily on the stone floor of the church, and he shouted furiously, 'Do you see my great legs, little man, my large feet, my sharp ------?' but before the buggane could finish the sentence, the tailor had put the finishing stitch into the breeches, and was running out of the church, for when he finally looked up he could see that the buggane was forcing up the roof beams with his enormous arms. Just as Timothy escaped from the church, the roof fell in with a crash. The fiendish laugh of the buggane echoed around the dust-filled ruins and Timothy fled in terror.

He could hear the frightful creature pounding along behind him, its huge jaws snapping at his heels, as if to swallow him whole. Timothy ran for miles and miles, chased by the hideous buggane, and leapt into Marown churchyard. Since it was holy ground, the buggane couldn't follow him there; but, in its rage, the angry creature ripped its own great head from its body, and threw it with

enormous force at the tailor's feet, where it exploded like a bomb, covering Timothy in sticky green goo. Amazingly, the tailor survived, though he was always a bit little jumpy, a little bit twitchy, after his experiences that night. He even won his bet and earned himself a fortune. Nobody complained about the last few stitches in the breeches being less tidy than the rest, after all ... how neatly would you sew with a horrible buggane rising up out of the floor in front of you?

As for the buggane, it wasn't seen again, but they never dared put another roof on St Trinian's church, in case the buggane came back.

This story, which appears in Sophia Morrison's *Manx Fairy Tales* (1911), is one of the best-known legends on the Isle of Man. It also appears in *The Folklore of the Isle of Man* by Margaret Killip (1975) and in *The Folklore of the Isle of Man* by A.W. Moore (1891).

This is my version of the story, but it does stick pretty closely to the original ... and the roofless church of St Trinian's can still be seen. Of course, this story is told from the point of view of Timothy the tailor, and the other humans involved. To understand it from the buggane's position, read on ...

THE BUGGANE'S TALE

I know what you think of me, you people who live on the Isle of Man. You've heard the story lots of times, haven't you? How the terrible buggane frightened poor Timothy the tailor and ripped the roof off St Trinian's church. You all think you know exactly what happened, but none of you have thought about it from my point of view, have you? Oh no, humans are far too self-centred for that.

Prejudiced, that's what humans are. Alright, so I don't look just like you ... I'm a little bigger ... or a lot bigger, depending what mood I'm in. So what if I have hooves instead of feet? At least I never get bunions! And claws are far more useful than fingers, especially for ripping people's heads off. Perhaps my teeth are a little pointier than yours, and my breath is rather toxic ... who cares? I'm not planning to advertise toothpaste, or kiss anyone, and nobody wants to kiss me, that's for sure. But have you *read* the descriptions of me? They make me sound like some kind of monster. And the *illustrations*! Bat's wings, ram's horns, the Devil's tail ... I mean, it's insulting! Have you any idea how hurtful it is to be misunderstood all the time? Well, it's time I told my side of the story!

There was a time, you know, when it was the humans on the Island who were in the minority, but frankly you humans breed like rabbits and soon there were more of you than there were of us magical creatures. You took over all the pleasant places, the peaceful coves, the dappled orchards, leaving us nowhere to go, driving us into the wilder parts of the Island, and even then you gave us no peace. Take me, for example, I rather liked it down in Laxey before you lot turned up, but you're so noisy ... hob-nailed boots and hammers, music and metal machines! Who can live like that? I moved out hundreds of years ago, to a quiet spot in the country. I just wanted a bit of peace and quiet ... I have very sensitive hearing you know ... and what happened? You followed me! I found a nice cavern under a sunny hillside and sank down into it, coming out now and then to nibble on a sheep or devour a stray child. Humans thought that the Little People stole the children away, but no, it was me. Well, a buggane has to eat, you know! Where was I? Oh yes, people ... they spread everywhere, soon some were living around the area I'd retreated to. And then ... *and then* ... they decided to build a church *right over* where I lived. A church! With clanging bells and chanting Christians just above my head! And they didn't ask me, oh no, they just built it. Haven't they heard of planning permission? I mean, I don't wish to be a NIMBY, but *I was here first*! I have rights too, you know, or at least I should have.

I started with a peaceful protest, pulling down a few roof beams when the church was almost finished ... I was quite considerate really, I didn't even touch the walls. Remarkably restrained of me. 'Controlled aggression' that's the term that's used these days, I believe. I may have chuckled as I did it, it was very satisfying, but to say I gave an evil laugh was a complete exaggeration! I was only doing what any modern council would ... taking down a building that was put up without permission. Well, the humans put the roof back on, and I pulled it down again. I may have laughed again, I can't recall, but it was very enjoyable, so perhaps I gave a little chuckle ... but I do *not* cackle! Frankly, I was getting pretty bored with the whole thing. Had these people no imagination? Well, it turned out one of them had. Somebody decided that they could stop me pulling down the church, just by having a person stay in the building overnight the next time that the roof was almost finished. They even had the bishop on standby to consecrate the place, and keep me out, the moment the last roof nail was hammered in, if their plan worked ... and it could have done, you know, if they'd gone about it the right way. If all the people who wanted the church built had spent the night in the almost completed church praying, I would have left them alone. The new religion, the Christian religion, is a powerful one … more powerful than you know. But perhaps I have more respect for your God than you do because the people didn't pray, did they? They didn't even all show up that night, the people who wanted the church. The cowards sent one young man, one feeble young man called Timothy, and he was only there for a bet! Now I ask you, is that any way to show respect for your God? Even if Timothy was broke, should he really have tried to make money out of protecting the church overnight? It seemed wrong to me!

I'll admit, I was a bit surprised when this weedy-looking young man crept into the church on the night the roof was nearly finished. He carried a candle and a lot of other bits and pieces, which he spread out all over the floor. At first I thought it was some new religious ritual and I kept my distance, but then I heard some of the locals talking outside the church, about how this Timothy was a tailor, and had said he could make a whole pair of trousers in one night, by hand, working by candlelight while he waited for me to show up. Well that was just insulting! If he was waiting for *me*, he should have been in there shaking with fear, and if he was really there to please his God and keep me away so the church could be finished, he should have been praying not sewing!

To give him his due, I expect he did want the church to be finished, but he wanted to make some money too. To me, that seemed disrespectful. Disrespectful of his God, and of me, and if there's one thing that makes me angry, it's when people don't show respect! And he shouldn't have made me angry … people don't like me when I'm angry. To be fair, I did wind him up a bit too. I waited until the night was nearly over, and he thought his plan had worked, and that I'd stayed away because he was there. Huh! As if! He also thought he'd get the trousers finished, but I was just playing with him. When he just had a hand's width of fabric left to sew, I started to make my appearance. Not all at one go, of course, but bit by bit, which was far more alarming.

I emerged silently, piece by piece, up through the floor of the church, just before dawn. I waited till my chin was above the ground before I spoke ... very loudly ... you should have seen that tailor jump! I yelled, 'See my great head, little man?' ... but he didn't see, did he? He was too busy sewing to look up and take any notice of me, so I carried on shouting, 'My large eyes, my sharp teeth?' ... I'd filed my teeth specially, to make them nice and pointy, but I might as well not have bothered, because *he wasn't looking at me!* He heard me though ... I could tell because his hands began to shake, the stitches he was sewing became untidy, the thread was pulled too tight making the material bunch up, he was *scared!*

I floated further up through the floor, until my chest and arms were free of the ground, and shouted even louder. 'See my great chest, little man, my large hands, my sharp nails?' The timid tailor was shaking with fear, but he still couldn't bring himself to look at me, he just said, 'I see, I see', while he *carried on sewing.* He didn't so much as glance up, so he never saw the rat's blood dripping from my fingernails, and that made me *annoyed.* I'd gone to a lot of effort over my appearance, and he couldn't even be bothered to look. He was still stitching away, determined to win his bet. As far as I was concerned, he was showing a total lack of respect, *and that made me angry!*

I wrenched the rest of my body up through the floor, till my carefully polished hooves were tapping lightly on the church's flag-stones and my tail was lashing in all directions. This time I roared *'See my great legs little man, my large hooves, my sharp tail?'* and finally ... finally ... he finished the last stitch and looked up. It was too late though; I'd had enough of being ignored. His lack of respect for me had made me even more angry and he shouldn't have made me angry ... as I said, people don't like me when I'm angry. I grew larger and larger, raised my arms up to the church roof, and began to rip it down. The tailor, still clutching the trou-sers, turned and fled towards the door, reaching it just as I brought the roof crashing to the ground. The little man looked so terrified that I couldn't help laughing ... but to describe the laugh as *fiendish* was a complete exaggeration!

My work was done, I had wrecked the church roof *again* ... I would have peace once more. It was time to return to my lair. And

then I saw the tailor ... running ... he was going so fast anybody would think I was chasing him, and he was still clutching those ridiculous trousers! It was outrageous, he hadn't protected the church from me at all, but he was still going to win his bet! The thought made my blood boil, and I raced after him. I wanted to get those trousers and tear them to shreds, but he had too much of a head start. Although I was catching him up, he'd run for several miles, reached the next village and was heading for another church. A church with a roof, a church that had been blessed ... a church *I could not enter!* I stretched out my hand to grab him, but he leapt over a wall and into the churchyard. He was standing on holy ground and I couldn't follow him. He turned and looked at me, *really* looked at me. Now he saw my sharpened teeth, my blood-tipped claws, my polished hooves ... although even then he wasn't really paying attention, he later described them as clawed feet! And he dared ... he *dared* to smile. Some people said it was a nervous smile ... relief at having survived the night ... but to me he looked *smug!*

How dare he look smug! Now you might have gathered that I have a bit of an anger management problem. On a good day I can be calm, laid back, relaxed ... but there aren't many good days, and this wasn't one of them. There was the tailor, still carrying the trousers, looking smug and standing on holy ground where I couldn't reach him ... where *he thought* I couldn't reach him. It made me so angry that I just could not let him get away with it. It made me so angry that I had to reach him. It made me so angry that I had to have revenge! It made me *so angry* that I raised my long strong arms with the sharp bloodied claws and I wrenched off my own head and flung it into the churchyard where it landed at the tailor's feet and exploded, spraying anger, rage and green gloop all over him.

I didn't see what happened next ... being headless is a *little* inconvenient ... but I heard that the tailor survived. He even won his bet, because he did get the trousers finished, just about, though I know for a fact that the last few stitches were not exactly neat! Frankly I don't think he deserved a single penny of the money ... and I can't *BELIEVE* they made *him* out to be a hero!

As for the church, they never dared to put a roof on it again, in case I reappeared to make more trouble ... though they rather hoped that by ripping my head off I'd caused my own death. They were wrong, of course. I'm still here. Even my head re-grew eventually, though it was never as good a fit as the one I threw away. So here I am, in my cavern beneath St Trinian's roofless church, enjoying peace, solitude and the odd rat snack (not so many stray children around these days), and wondering what to do next. I'm getting bored, I feel the need for a little entertainment ... I rather enjoyed ripping down that roof. Anyone need a demolition expert?

೨೦

This is my own twist on the legend of 'The Buggane of St Trinian's' and it owes nothing to any source except the original story, and my imagination ... but it is fun to tell!

೨೦

THE MAN IN THE FROCK

Glashtins are small, hairy goblin-like creatures that are always causing mischief, one way or another, though they can make themselves useful too. Adult glashtins are pretty clever fellows, crafty and full of tricks, but not even magical creatures come into the world fully formed. Everything was young once, and young-sters make mistakes.

A long time ago there were sheep in the folds down near the Calf of Man, and one night an old man forgot to put his sheep away safely. He sent his son out to do the job when it was fully dark, and the lad came in to say he'd got all the sheep into the fold alright, but there were two or three lambs out there, leaping about, and making mischief. The old man knew at once that these 'lambs' were young glashtin, which had been attracted to the flock because of the sheep being left out of the fold. The old man also knew that very soon, when they weren't causing trouble with the sheep, these creatures would start chasing after the girls on the farm. He felt it was his fault they were there, because his forgetfulness had attracted their attention, so if anyone got hurt, he would be to blame. Some folk said that he should make the most of having the glashtins there, for the creatures were strong, and would help with the farm work at night if they chose to, but he knew they'd cause a lot of trouble for the women.

Sure enough, a few days later one of these hairy little creatures caught one of the girls, and had hold of her dress by the back of her skirt, but like all young things, he needed a nap, so he sat down and fell asleep, still gripping the young woman's clothing. The girl was scared at first, but she had her sewing scissors in her pocket, so once she was sure he was deeply asleep, she reached behind her and cut away the part of her dress that the glashtin was clutching. She ran off with a big, and rather embarrassing, hole in the back of her skirt, but even though her dignity was in tatters, she herself was safe enough, and proud of her quick wits. When the young glashtin woke up, all he held in his hand was a large scrap of fabric, which he threw over his shoulder with a curse.

Well, the old man wanted to get rid of these young creatures before they grew strong enough to cause serious harm. So one night he sent all the women to bed early, partly to keep them safe, and partly so that they wouldn't poke fun at him. Once he was sure that everyone was safely out of the way, he put on a cap and a woman's dress. He even added some hanks of sheep's fleece, sticking out from under the cap, like an old lady's hair. He felt like a fool when he looked in the mirror, but it had to be done!

Usually a man in a frock is seen as a figure of fun, like the dame in a pantomime, but this man had a serious purpose. He sat down by the fire, pulled out the spinning wheel, and began to spin some yarn. It was not work that he usually did, so he wasn't very good at it. The young glashtins crept in through the door, watching in fascination. Soon they began to ask, 'Are you turning the wheel? Are you doing it right?' They had never seen a woman make such a mess of her spinning. Mind you, they'd never seen a woman who looked like this either … large and lumpen, in spite of the dress, with rough skin and straggly hair showing under her cap. Most

women on the Island took pride in their appearance, be they plain
or pretty, old or young, it was one of the reasons that glashtins
were attracted to them, but this one ... well, they didn't know
what to make of her, and their curiosity drew them closer.

The young glashtins started to call out to the woman at the
wheel. 'Comb your hair,' said one.

'Tie it back with a ribbon,' remarked another.

'Then it won't get in your eyes and you can see to spin,' called
the third.

'Your dress needs a sash, to give it some shape.'

'Your boots are too clumpy, ladies wear dainty shoes.'

'Your skin is all rough, you should make it softer.'

On and on went the glashtins, offering their advice ... for
they liked girls and women, and knew how they should be.
They couldn't bear the rough and ready state of the woman at the
spinning wheel, and wanted to give her a makeover ... and with
every piece of advice they gave the creatures crept closer.

There was a grown-up glashtin outside, keeping an eye on the
young ones from a distance, and he knew that the figure at the
wheel was not a woman at all, but the old man. This glashtin
called out to the younger ones, warning them, and telling them to
come away, but of course, they wouldn't listen. Youngsters never
do, do they? Now in that cottage they burned turf on the fire,
and when the young glashtins had crept close enough, the old man
reached out and used the fire tongs to grab a smouldering turf off
the fire, and threw it over the creatures, and burned them, and the
glashtins made a terrible fuss before running out of the cottage.

Their shouting and crying woke up the rest of the household,
and into the room ran the old man's son, and his wife, and his
daughters, and the girl who helped on the farm, and every
single one of them saw the old man in his feminine disguise.
They couldn't help laughing, for he looked so silly, but they didn't
tease him too much, because he had found a way to get rid of the
glashtins, and the creatures never came back.

Now when it comes to folklore, you can hit the odd snag and for me, that's the trouble with glashtins. In some stories, possibly more recent ones, they appear to be similar to the cabbyl-ushtey, the water horse (of which, more later), but in others they are a type of brownie, or a hairy goblin, or a sprite, and that's what they are in this old tale, which can be found in *The Folklore of the Isle of Man* by A.W. Moore (1891).

THE DARK STRANGER

This is the story about a glashtin, a water horse. Now I know what you're thinking … you've just heard about the little, hairy, goblin-like glashtin in another story, and they didn't sound like water horses to you. You know this because you were paying attention. You've also heard somewhere about water horses on the Island, and they are called cabbyl-ushtey, and are dangerous creatures that live in rivers, ponds and streams. But in some stories the glashtin seem to be water horses too; they too are dangerous creatures but *these* water horses live in the sea. They can change from man to horse and back again, and they prowl around the countryside at night, looking for pretty young girls to devour and destroy.

Maggie was a pretty young girl and she was alone at the cottage one day. Her father had gone to the market in Douglas and wasn't yet home, so the girl got on with her chores. She milked the cow and fed the chickens and gave extra grain to the little cockerel that they were fattening up for their Christmas dinner. Then she heard strange hollow groans and the sound of a horn in the distance. It was blown by the dooiney-oie, the night-man … a mournful creature, who blew his horn to give those on the Island warning of approaching storms. Maggie knew that it was always worth taking the dooiney-oie's warnings seriously, so she put the cow in their little barn, and shut the chickens in the hen house, but she could not catch the cockerel to put him away, so she decided he'd have to take his chances with the weather, and shelter in the tiny porch if the storm was bad.

Then she went inside, lit the fire, laid the table, and prepared a meal, ready for her father's return. A terrible storm did indeed break over the Island, so bad that her father decided to stay in Douglas that night, rather than make the long journey home in such awful weather.

Back at the cottage, Maggie waited for her father. She waited and waited, becoming more and more worried about him. Then, late at night, she heard three loud knocks on the heavy wooden door. She opened it to find a stranger standing there. He was a handsome, well-dressed young man, with curly black hair and dark, flashing eyes. He was also soaked to the skin. Her father always told her not to let strangers into the house when she was there alone, but the Manx are a hospitable people – how could she leave the young man out in such a dreadful storm? She led him into the cottage and settled him by the fire to warm himself, and let his wet clothes dry. She offered him some supper, but he wouldn't accept anything … although as she washed up her own plate at the sink, she noticed out of the corner of her eye that he took some lumps of sugar from the bowl on the table and an apple from the shelf by the door and she began to grow suspicious. Horses eat sugar lumps, horses eat apples … surely a normal person would just have accepted the food she'd offered?

Finally the young man lay down on a blanket beside the fire and went to sleep. The girl crept closer to him and blew gently at the hair around his ears. In the dim firelight she could see that the ears were long and pointed, like horses' ears … not rounded like human ones at all. Then she knew that this was a glashtin. At any moment he could wake up, take the form of a horse and drag her into the sea to devour and destroy her. She longed for the little cockerel outside to crow, for that would signal that dawn had broken and the glashtin would have no power over her in the daylight … but morning was some hours away yet, so all she could do was stay as still as possible. Perhaps, if she didn't disturb him, he would sleep until morning, and his power over her would be gone. She didn't dare creep out of the cottage in case her movements woke the creature up.

A great crash of thunder wakened the glashtin a couple of hours later, and Maggie quaked with fear. The young man sat up and

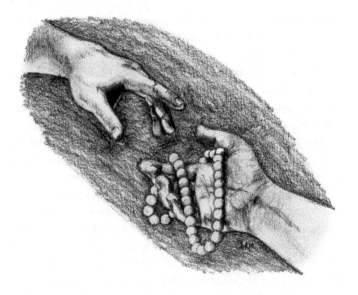

turned his head slowly to look at the girl, who started to back away from him. Wanting to draw her closer to him, he pulled a string of pearls out of his pocket and held it in front of her, hoping she would reach out to touch them so he could grab her wrist. Instead, she leapt up from her chair and ran to the door, pulling it open. She was determined to escape, but the glashtin had reached the door almost as quickly as she had and he grabbed her arm. She screamed in fright, so loudly that she woke the cockerel, which was sleeping just outside, in the shelter of the porch.

Thinking it was morning, the creature started to crow, and the glashtin let go of Maggie's arm and began to run. He knew he had to be back in the sea by daybreak. Maggie watched as he changed shape ... first his body altered into that of a horse, leaving a human head on his shoulders, with sharp teeth and long pointed ears. It was the creepiest thing Maggie had ever seen. Then the head too shifted into the form of a horse, and the glashtin galloped away.

The storm faded with the dawn, and by lunchtime Maggie's father had returned. When she told him what had happened, he made her promise never to open the door to a stranger again while he was away at the market. He also agreed that the little cockerel should be rewarded for tricking the glashtin into thinking it was dawn. The bird was to live a long and happy life, and never end up as Christmas dinner, because he had saved Maggie's life.

꙰

The glashtin has become my bête noire in this book, because of its blurry definitions. As far as I can gather, the hairy goblin is the traditional glashtin and the water horse has been given the name more recently. This is where it all seems to get a little bit confusing. Cabbyl-ushtey are water horses and glashtin, in this and some other stories, are water horses, but they seem to behave differently. The only way I can make sense of it is to think of them as two different species of water horses, which behave differently and live in separate environments.

So, the glashtin are water horses that live in the sea, and come ashore at night in human form to find beautiful young women, and then drag them back into the sea to devour and destroy them. The cabbyl-ushtey, as far as I can work out, are fresh-water horses, which live in rivers, ponds and steams. They too try to attract people to follow them into the water, and drown, but they don't change into human form.

However, on page 39 of *The Folklore of the Isle of Man* published in 1891, A.W. Moore says, 'The Glashtin or Glashan combine the attributes of the Scotch Brownies and the Scandinavian Troll, though the glashtin seems to be a water-horse also ...', so perhaps it's not such a recent confusion and the glashtin as a water horse is therefore not just a modern invention.

I've included this story because I love it, and I hope I'm not treading on too many Manx toes by adding it to the collection.

Glashtin and cabbyl-ushtey are both mentioned in *The Folklore of the Isle of Man* by A.W. Moore (1891) and a story about one occurs in 'The Glashtin of Derbyhaven' in *The Green Glass Bottle – Folk Tales from The Isle of Man* by Zena Carus (1975).

꙰

The 'dooiney-oie', which I have woven into my version of this tale, crops up in both *The Folklore of the Isle of Man* by A.W. Moore (1891) and *Manx Fairy Tales* by Sophia Morrison (1911). This version of the glashtin (or glastyn) is also described in *Fables, Fantasies and Folklore of the Isle of Man* by Henry Penrice (1996).

THE LONELY KEIMAGH

The keimagh was terribly lonely. His mournful, ugly face was wet with tears of sorrow. Not that there was anyone there to see it. He hardly saw a soul these days. His job was to guard the dead in the churchyard, and he never left his post. He wasn't guarding the graves from interference by other humans ... although his gloomy presence sometimes frightened them away too. No, the keimagh was a gentle spirit, and his job was to protect the graveyard from other spirits on the Island ... fiercer magical creatures like the buggane, the glashtin, and the tarroo-ushtey ... and he had done his job well over the years. Nothing had disturbed the quiet dreams of the dead. They rested in peace, but the keimagh himself was not so happy.

Times had changed, the old church within the graveyard was forgotten and in ruins. The churchyard was full and no new burials had taken place there for many years. The church had once been the centre point of a small village, but that too had been empty and abandoned for years. The humans had moved to be nearer the town and the ancient cottages were beginning to fall down.

The keimagh felt he couldn't leave the old place, but he wasn't sure that there was any point in staying. There didn't seem to be many magical creatures left on the Island to defend the graveyard from, but it felt wrong to abandon his work and leave. Besides, he had no idea where else to go. He wasn't really sure what was happening in other parts of the Island. Outside the wall of the churchyard grew an elder tree ... often called a trammon tree. It had been planted in the garden of a cottage on the other side of the wall many years ago, to keep witches away, and for the fairies, the Little People, to play in. Once, the tiny creatures had kept the keimagh company, calling out to him from the branches of the tree at night. Now they never came to visit him, though their ears were still attached to the base of the tree. These were flesh-coloured, almost transparent, the size and shape of a little child's ears.

Humans believed that the Little People would leave their ears (or lugs) behind them when they went underground at dawn, to keep themselves informed of what was going on in the world during daylight hours. A few years ago, a man who knew all

about plants came to look at that trammon tree. The keimagh had heard him telling the people who were with him that 'Fairy-lugs and fairies'-ears are names for the fleshy fungus which grows only on the stem of the Trammon or Elder-tree.' The man said that they weren't magical at all, just some kind of mush-room, but the keimagh was a creature of magic himself, and he knew otherwise.

Every few days he would wander over to the wall and call out the news to the fairy ears ... not that there *was* much news, just that he was still there, the graves were still undisturbed, the village was deserted and he was *so very lonely*. He wasn't sure if the Little People were still listening but then, one night, he found out that they were taking notice of what he told them.

He had dozed off in the darkness and awoke to hear a soft, shuffling sound, and saw movement in the moonlight, in amongst the headstones. He could only see a shadowy outline, but it looked to him like another keimagh! And it sounded like a female, weeping.

'Excuse me,' asked the keimagh gently. 'Are you alright?'

'I am now,' she said, staring at him in amazement. 'The Little People told me I would find you here. The graveyard I used to guard has been dug up, to make way for a new road. The bodies I had protected were moved to another place ... a new place where I couldn't follow. There was none of the old magic there. I was left with nowhere to go. I thought I was doomed to wither away and disappear forever, but then one of the Little People found me. They told me that they'd heard you were still here and would welcome company, and so ... here I am.'

'And you are most welcome,' he said. 'You are *more* than welcome to stay here with me and help me guard my dead.' He looked at her face in the moonlight ... she too had a sorrowful, ugly face, like all keimaghs, but to him she was beautiful. He had never heard of a graveyard guarded by two keimaghs before ... but the world was changing, why shouldn't they change with it? He was content to know that the Little People had heard him, when he spoke to their ears on the Trammon tree, and now he would have company. The two keimaghs would watch over the graveyard together … and need never be lonely again.

≈

This is another new story. The keimagh is mentioned in *The Folklore of the Isle of Man* by A.W. Moore (1891) and his role protecting graveyards crops up in *Fables, Fantasies and Folklore of the Isle of Man* by Harry Penrice (1996). The role of the Trammon tree is referenced in *The Folklore of the Isle of Man* by Margaret Killip (1975). However, I couldn't find any actual stories to tell about this fascinating creature, so in the end I created this one, trying to weave two strands of Manx folklore together.

8

Extraordinary People

The Magician's Palace

In the days of enchantment there was a great wizard on the Island. This was not the Lord Manannan; at this point *he* had been exiled by St Patrick, leaving the land open to other magics. Now *this* magician, who was not a good man, had used his power to create for himself the most magnificent palace that people on the Isle of Man had ever seen, or so the legend tells us.

Not that they *did* see it, because, when people went to look for it, whether to catch a glimpse of its splendour or steal some of the wizard's wealth, they were immediately turned to stone once they got too close to the building. Even those people who just came searching near the palace for their missing relatives were turned to stone themselves as they climbed among the granite rocks scattered around the palace. Soon the magician's palace was surrounded by stone shapes, like statues. The area looked like the entrance to the Gorgon's lair (or one of those modern garden centres that concentrates more on sculptures than on plants ... you know the sort I mean. You can buy five different designs of stone dragons, but you can't buy a rhubarb plant for love nor money!). This wizard, for some reason, hated humans, though we may never know why. He was human himself, we know that much, but no more. Perhaps he was bullied as a child, perhaps he never got picked for games; whatever the reason, he learned to hate, and he did hating very well indeed. Because of this, there were no human servants at the palace; instead he was served by infernal spirits.

People came to think of him as the terror of the Island, and for years they stopped going anywhere near the place. Then one day something changed. It wasn't the wizard, as far as we know. He seemed unchanging ... though as nobody had seen him for years, I'm not quite sure how people knew.

What changed was that the wizard had a visitor. It was an accident of course ... nobody would have gone near the wizard's palace on purpose. A poor wandering man, who was almost a pilgrim, was travelling around the Island on foot. He survived by offering to do odd jobs for the cottagers, and in return they would give him some food to eat. He was a good and Godly man, and the arrangement suited him. His needs were simple, just a little food, and shelter in bad weather, so why cloud things by the exchange of money? That was the way he saw it.

He was from the south of the Island and somehow he had never heard tell of this wizard or his palace. By now people avoided the place and didn't speak of it, for fear of encouraging foolish young-sters to go exploring the place and be turned to stone.

This old man was walking up near the wizard's palace, on Barrule Mountain, and was surprised that all the cottages in that area were deserted and in ruins, for no one wanted to live there anymore. There wasn't a soul to offer him shelter or a bite to eat, and a harsh wind was blowing across the mountain. Night was coming and the old man wandered on, worried that he'd have to sleep on the cold mountainside. He'd done it before, often enough, but not in such harsh weather. The wind was getting fiercer now; soon it would be blowing a gale.

He kept walking, hoping to find somewhere sheltered to sleep until, as the light was fading, he saw the palace up ahead of him, and at first he was delighted.

It was like something out of a dream, built of shining marble, and with great doors covered in gold. The doors were open, as if to invite visitors in, but something about it felt wrong to the old man. He didn't want to go and wander in, or knock on those doors and trouble the servants. The bigger the house the colder the welcome, in his experience, and he had no wish to be moved on before morning. He didn't even want to get too close to the shining walls of the palace. Something about the great stones scattered around the building worried him, their shapes were rather too human for his liking. Once he'd allowed that chilling thought to cross his mind, he couldn't get rid of the idea.

Using his tinderbox, he lit a little dry stick, and reached this flickering light towards the nearest block of stone, while keeping well back from it himself. His blood ran cold when he recognised the features of the stone figure. Surely that was little Neddy Hom, a dwarf who had gone missing the year before? But who would take the time to carve a statue of Neddy? He wasn't a hero, or a rich merchant, he was just an ordinary workingman, and if somebody did go to all that trouble, why leave it lying on the ground?

The old man took a step back, and then another step back, until he couldn't see the face of the statue any more. He wished he could just walk away, but now it was full dark, and only a fool would walk on the mountain at night. He would have to stay there until morning. At least the bulk of the palace blocked some of the force of the gale, he thought, as he settled down on the ground, though the wind was still swirling this way and that around him. He wasn't expecting to get much sleep under the circumstances, but the least he could do to help himself get through the night was to have a bite of supper. The last cottager he'd done a few jobs for had sent him off with a small parcel of cooked meat, and a hunk of bread. He felt in his pocket for the food, for the flaming stick had burnt to nothing, but when he pulled it out and took a bite, of meat and bread together, it seemed a little tasteless. Of course the flavour of a food might come from the company in which it's eaten, or the surroundings of the diner, and there wasn't much the old man could do about either of those things ... but he could add a little salt. That would improve the taste, alright. He pulled a twist of paper out of his other pocket, and opened it up. Inside was a small portion of salt.

He took a pinch of the salt between his fingers, sprinkling it on to his food, but before he could close up the paper and put the salt safely back in his pocket, a gust of wind caught it, plucking it from his fingers and carrying it through the air towards the palace. In the moonlight he could see that the salt was scattered across the granite boulders, and the paper, with the last few crystals in it, landed upside down on the ground at the very entrance to the palace, where the golden doors stood open.

Within moments he started to hear terrible groans and wails, coming from the very ground itself, the gale became a hurricane, lightning slashed the sky and thunder rolled over his head. Suddenly the magnificent palace broke into a thousand pieces, which were scattered to the four winds. Even the boulders that were spread across the ground vanished from sight.

The old man found himself out in the open, surrounded by nothing more than empty mountainside. He dropped the remains of his supper and knelt in prayer, grateful to have survived this strange adventure. He had no doubt now that the boulders really had once been real people, and that if he had gone even a few steps closer to the palace, he too would have been turned to stone. He continued to pray, and thank God for his deliverance from such a terrible fate, until the sun rose over the mountain.

Then he hurried to the next village and told them what had happened. Of course, at first they were slow to believe him, this strange old man telling an even stranger story. Eventually, however, they agreed to go with him to the spot, which some of them had glimpsed in the past, and seeing both the palace and the boulders gone, they had no choice but to accept his story. Grateful to have been set free of such a terrible wizard, they joined with the old man in prayers of thanksgiving.

Talking through what had happened, people came to the conclusion that it was the salt spilt on the ground that had broken the magician's power and made the palace disappear, and because of that, salt became so significant that nobody would go out on any important business without taking some in their pockets.

In fact, they wouldn't move house, or marry, or make any special arrangements, without salt being exchanged. Indeed, it became the custom that a beggar in the streets would only accept food if salt was offered with it, as a sign of goodwill and additional benevolence.

⁊

This story is in *The Folklore of the Isle of Man* by A. W. Moore (1891), and in *Manx Fairy Tales* by Sophia Morrison (1911). Also found in *More Manx Myths* by Dennis W. Turner (2005).

Salt has had an important role in many superstitious ceremonies. The high priest of the Jews was ordered to season all offerings with salt. The Egyptians and Romans also used it in their sacrifices. In Ireland, before the seed was put into the ground, salt was sent into the field for the purpose of counteracting the power of the witches and fairies.

So, on the Isle of Man, salt was placed in the churn lest the fairies should prevent the production of butter. Also, in the past, salt was placed on the breasts of corpses on the Island, as elsewhere, as a symbol of the immortality of the soul. The dread of spilling salt was a general superstition, though in this case, it was the spilling of salt that destroyed the magician's palace, and so could be said to have been a good thing.

THE DEEMSTER'S TALE

Now a Deemster, on the Island, is a type of judge, and this is the story of one who was very dedicated to his profession, and to justice. Centuries ago this Deemster got a message, while he was in Ramsey, in the north of the Island, that he was needed back in Castletown in the south as quickly as possible. There was a girl whose case he was pleading, and the time had come for her trial. It was unexpectedly scheduled for the next morning, and he had to be there, to be sure that she had somebody to speak on her behalf.

⁊

It was winter, and as he saddled his horse he knew he'd have a hard journey of it, for snow was already on the ground and more was falling. His friends tried to persuade him not to go, saying that surely the girl could get someone else to speak up for her, but the Deemster understood her case and felt he had a better chance of proving her innocence than anyone else. He hated the idea of a woman who had committed no crime suffering all the indignities of a prison cell, and was determined to get her out as quickly as possible. He knew his duty and wasn't about to let somebody down for the sake of his own convenience.

It was only a twenty-mile journey, but on horseback, in winter, it would be a difficult one. The shortest route was over Snaefell Mountain, which could be hazardous at the best of times, but that was the route he took, being determined to get there in time. Up on the mountain the track was hidden by snow, and a blizzard began to rage, making the journey even harder.

He'd ridden about twelve miles, and thought that East Baldwin must be up ahead. Perhaps he could find shelter there and carry on when the wind dropped, though he was reluctant to delay his journey at all. His horse, though, was exhausted and he knew the poor creature needed rest. He *thought* he was still on the right path, an ancient packhorse road, but in the blizzard it was hard to be sure. However, he and the horse were indeed lost, and on the rough ground they were now crossing, the horse stumbled and fell, bringing his rider down with him. They were already bitterly cold, and now too winded and too weak to get back to their feet. The snow continued to fall, blanketing them both, and the bitter weather killed them.

Down in Castletown the girl's trial began with no one to speak for her, but the judge postponed it until she could get help. By that time the Deemster's body had been discovered, as the wind blew away the snow covering it. Word was carried to Castletown and the girl wept that his journey on her behalf should have caused his tragic death. When eventually she was proved innocent and released, she insisted on travelling to the spot where the Deemster had died. She built a cairn there in his memory, which stood for many years, but eventually, when a dry stone wall was built across the piece of ground where the cairn stood, the memorial was changed. The outline of a man, in white quartz stones, was built into the wall itself, in memory of his deed, and even when the wall became unstable, and had to be rebuilt, 'The White Man of Baldwin' was reconstructed too. It remains as a lasting tribute to a respected man of law, who gave his life to try and see justice done.

❧

This tale appears in *More Manx Myths* by Dennis W. Turner (2005). The wall itself, with the figure marked out in it, still exists and can be seen, though you'd need a good pair of walking boots to get to it.

JACK THE GIANT KILLER

(No actual giants were killed in the telling of this story)

There was once a boy called Jack, who thought that he was tough. He lived in a glen at the north end of the Island. His father was a fisherman, and mostly away at sea, and his mother had everything to do in the house and on the land, so the boy and his brothers were left to do pretty much as they liked. This was understandable, but it was his mother's first mistake … because what Jack liked to do was *fight*. He was always fighting with his brothers.

When he was four years old, he fought with the chickens … and beat them … not that chickens are exactly fierce! And his mother said, 'Aren't you clever and aren't you strong!' This was his mother's second mistake.

When he was six years old, he fought with the ducks … and beat them … not that ducks are exactly fierce either, especially as he was getting bigger and the ducks were still duck-sized. And his mother said, 'Aren't you clever and aren't you strong, but it's time to stop beating up the poultry now, Jack,' though she said it rather quietly, which was her third mistake.

When he was eight years old, he fought with the lambs ... and beat them ... though it was hardly a fair fight, as Jack was big for his age. His mother said, 'That's enough now, Jack,' under her breath, but Jack barely heard her, which was yet another mistake.

When he was ten years old, he fought with the goat ... and beat him ... although he only won because by now he had started to carry a big stick! And his mother didn't say very much at all ... she didn't like the look of the big stick any more than the goat did. This was her next mistake.

By the time he was twelve years old, he was as big as a man, and strong with it, and he was convinced that he could beat anyone in a fight ... animal or human. People started to come from all over the area to test their strength against him ... and he always won! His mother said, very quietly, that it was time he started to behave himself, but he didn't listen. Because of all the mistakes she'd made when he was younger, he'd stopped listening to her years ago, but she still worried about him.

By the time he was fourteen he had fought with everyone in the area, and not just with boys of his own age, oh no! He challenged *everyone* to a fight ... grannies coming home from the market and little children on their way to their first day at school. He was a nightmare, and everyone tried to avoid the boy and his big stick. These days they'd have given him an ASBO, but back then they just gave him a nickname ... Jack the Giant Killer, because he would fight anything. His mother gave up talking to him altogether, because he never listened to her anyway. As for Jack, he loved his new name, just as much as he would have loved having an actual giant to fight with. After all, he was sure he could win every battle he fought.

As far as his mother could see, the boy was only good for one thing ... catching wild pigs, or purrs, as they were called. There was always plenty of bacon on their table.

Now you may not think it, but pigs can be pretty fierce, and there was one old wild boar called the Purr Mooar, which was the terror of the district, and attacked anyone out walking alone. People had started to travel in twos and threes to protect themselves. Between Jack and the wild boar, everyone in the area was having a difficult time of it. Now Jack was determined to kill this purr, and set out with his big stick to look for him. He found the creature at last; cooling himself in a river, for it was a very warm day.

When the boar saw Jack, it gave a terrible roar and rushed at him. The boy hit the boar with his stick and the animal rolled over. Thinking it was dead, Jack began to dance around triumphantly, shouting, 'I've killed the wild boar! I've killed the wild boar!' He hadn't, for the boar scrambled to its feet and charged at Jack again, who hit at it a second time, causing it to fall. Convinced this time that it was dead, Jack began to dance around again, shouting, 'I've killed the wild boar! I've killed the wild boar!' But he was wrong

once more, for the boar was on its feet and charging at him. With a final blow Jack killed the creature, and shouted for the last time, 'I've killed the wild boar! I've killed the wild ... ooooh!' The boy looked down to discover that on the boar's third charge its tusk had ripped open his leg, cutting him down to the bone. Jack was weak with loss of blood and it took him hours to crawl home. His leg became infected and although he recovered it never healed properly. He had to turn his big stick into a crutch, and limped for the rest of his life.

Everyone came round and congratulated Jack, and said that they were grateful to him for killing the wild boar that had caused them so much trouble. Secretly, they were grateful to the wild boar as well, for injuring Jack the Giant Killer, and slowing him down a little ... for now he couldn't pick fights with people all the time, and the neighbourhood was a quieter and more peaceful place from then on ... much to Jack's mother's relief!

This story has a modern feel, but actually comes from *The Folklore of the Isle of Man* by A.W. Moore (1891). In the original, the boy was called Juan until he got his nickname of Jack the Giant Killer, but I use Jack throughout, because younger children found the name change confusing.

THE MALICIOUS SPIRIT

Jenny never set out to become a scaa goanlyssagh, a malicious ghost or spirit, really she didn't. All Jenny did was fall in love, with a charming young man called Liam. He told her he loved her, and wanted to marry her, and that they'd be together forever. At first she couldn't believe that such a handsome fellow could fall for an ordinary girl like her. They lived in the same village, so she knew that there were prettier girls that could have caught his eye ... and yet here he was, wanting to marry *her*.

She wanted to marry him too, of course ... in fact she thought
of little else. She adored her handsome lover ... and they did
become lovers, long before they were married. He was a very per-
suasive young man, and where was the harm, with the wedding
coming up? The harm, of course, made itself known soon after,
in the form of a bump, around her middle, that everyone soon
saw, and guessed the cause of. Despite the shame, Jenny was
excited, and thought that Liam would be too, but when she told
him, he didn't seem to be as thrilled as she was, although they'd
talked of having children, later on. He never suggested bringing
forward the date of the wedding ... and he came to visit her less
often after that. In fact, within a few weeks, he stopped coming
to see her at all.

Jenny cried herself to sleep every night, especially when she saw
him walking out with another girl. She had to face the truth, that
he had abandoned her. If Jenny's mother asked her how she slept,
she wept and said that she couldn't sleep at all, but that wasn't
strictly true. She would fall into an exhausted, tearful sleep in the
early hours of the morning, tossing and turning, her head filled
with thoughts of Liam.

And in the early hours of the morning, strange things began to
happen in Liam's cottage, at the other end of the village. He got up
early to go to his work, and went to get his clean shirt out of the
drawer in his bedroom. When he pulled the shirt from the drawer,
it fell from his fingers in bits, just as if it had been snipped apart
with scissors. Liam couldn't understand it, especially since he kept
his good clothes in a locked drawer, to prevent his younger brothers borrowing his things without permission. He swore and cursed,
but couldn't think how it could have happened.

A few nights later, Liam woke before dawn to find that he was
aching all over. He could feel someone pinching and nipping at
him, and bruises were starting to appear already ... and yet nobody
was in the room with him. He was beginning to feel frightened
now, and couldn't understand what was happening.

The following morning, when he went downstairs to have some
food before going to work, he found his mother stirring up some

porridge for them all. Liam took his place at the table and glanced outside. The sun was barely up and he yearned for the longer days of summer, when he could walk to work in the light. His mother turned round to fill the bowls with porridge, and screamed, pointing at Liam with her wooden spoon. He looked down and realised that his shirt was being chopped into pieces, even while he was wearing it. He couldn't feel anything or anyone, and his skin wasn't touched, but it was as if his clothes were being cut up with invisible scissors, and it terrified him. He watched, mesmerised, as little scrapes of fabric fell on to the floor and the table, while unseen hands cut up the shirt.

His mother insisted that they needed to get advice, and sent him to ask a local wise woman. When she heard what had happened to him over the last few mornings, she said he was being haunted by a scaa goanlyssagh ... the vengeful spirit of a living person. He asked if such a creature was a witch, but was told that they weren't, for they had no power to do lasting harm ... and probably wouldn't wish to. The wise woman said that if he knew who might wish him harm, he could call out their name when he was under attack, and that would drive them away.

The next morning, as Liam lay in his bed, the pinching and prodding started again ... and it hurt. He started to think through who might have a grudge against him, and called out a name. 'Mary?' he shouted, but the torment went on. 'Susan?' Still he was being pinched and prodded. 'Jenny?' he called, and the nipping stopped. 'Leave me alone, Jenny!' he shouted ... and in her room at the other end of the village, Jenny started awake, unsure why she had heard a voice calling her name.

Liam told his mother what the wise woman had said ... and that the trouble had stopped when he called out Jenny's name. Now Liam's mother was no fool, and asked him what reason the girl would have to want revenge on him. Liam told her the truth, and she said that he should honour his promise and marry the girl, but Liam refused. He had long since lost interest in Jenny. In that case, his mother insisted, he must go away, but send money back to support the child. She thought if he was out of sight then

Jenny would eventually forget about him, and haunt him no more. It would be better for everyone.

Jenny was heartbroken when Liam left the village, and had no idea that she had been the cause. If anyone had told her that she had turned into a vengeful spirit every night, she wouldn't have believed them, especially as she still loved Liam with all her heart. It just goes to show the power of love … for good or ill.

꿍

Scaa goanlyssagh appear in *William Cashen's Manx Folklore* by William Cashen (1912).

THE EFFIGY

In a lonely part of the north of the Island stood the cottage of an old woman, who had long been suspected of being a witch, and many of her neighbours claimed to have suffered by her 'black arts'.

One night a brave young man named Davy was walking home. It was late, for he had been to visit his mother, who was ill. By the time he had made sure that she'd had some supper, and everything else she needed, it was almost midnight. Most people would have avoided the old woman's cottage, even in the daylight, but at night? Not a soul would go near it in the dark!

Davy, however, needed to get home, for he had to be up early the next day for work, so he took the shortest route, and that led him right past the old lady's window. He did hesitate for a moment before setting off down that particular path, but he pulled himself together. He told himself that the stories he'd heard about the old woman *were* just stories, and that he should put his trust in God.

As he neared her cottage he saw that it was blazing with light, at a time when most folk were tucked up in bed. Curious, Davy couldn't resist peering in through a gap in the sacking that the old lady used as curtaining. What he saw alarmed him, for there was

the woman holding an image, like a dolly, in her hands ... though this dolly was dressed as a man. She was turning this object round and round in front of the fire, sticking pins into it occasionally, while she muttered some words over and over again ... though Davy couldn't understand what she said.

Davy sneezed, and the old lady dropped the dolly and turned her head to look in his direction, but he ducked down and she never saw his face. He hurried home, thankful to have escaped, for he was now convinced that she truly was a witch. When he woke up in the morning, the news was all around the village where he was staying to be near his work.

It seemed that the minister of the church had had a series of seizures the night before, and been burning up with fever – at around the time that Davy was peering in through the old lady's window – then, as suddenly as it had started, the minister's seizures stopped. Davy wondered if that had been the moment when he sneezed and distracted the old lady. The young man felt he had to tell somebody what he'd seen, so he went and spoke to the captain of the parish. The captain searched the woman's cottage and found the supposed effigy of the minister, along with a container full of rusty nails, pins, and skewers.

The old woman, now firmly identified as a witch, was put on trial and found guilty. She was sentenced to execution, but seemed quite untroubled by her fate as she walked to the place where she was going to be burnt at the stake. She even confessed to the crime for which she was about to suffer. She saw that the captain of the parish was going to consign the image of the minister to the flames, along with the woman who had created it, and a grin twisted her features. The captain hesitated and Davy, who had come, along with most of the villagers, to witness her execution, removed the figure from the captain's fingers and tucked it into his own pocket for safekeeping. The witch went up in flames and every-one breathed a sigh of relief. Everyone except Davy, who realised that *he* was now responsible for the effigy of the minister. The old woman might be dead, but there was still a chance that the little figure was cursed, and whatever happened to it would also happen to the minister. Davy would now have to keep the figure safe, for the rest of the minister's life.

❧

A version of this story is found in *The Folklore of the Isle of Man* by A.W. Moore (1891).

BURIED TREASURE

There was once a man called Johnny, who lived on the Isle of Man, and he met one of the Little People. Johnny was on his way back from the pub at the time, and he was singing, as people sometimes do. A few of the villagers called out from their cottages for him to shut up, for they were trying to sleep, but one person didn't want him to be quiet, for he was enjoying the music. This, of course, was one of Themselves, who was following along behind Johnny, trying to learn the tune he was singing. As Johnny weaved along he tripped over a stone on the path and landed flat on his face in the mud. He heard someone laughing nearby and when he looked up, there was a little man, grinning at him.

'You've given me a good evening's entertainment,' said the little man, 'so I'll give you something in return. If you get yourself to London Bridge, in London Town, across the sea, and start to dig, you'll find a fortune.' The little man vanished and Johnny was left to make his own, rather wobbly, way home.

In the morning he told his wife what the little man had said to him ... but of course, she didn't believe him. 'You were drunk,' she said. 'You imagined the whole thing,' she said. 'How could you get to London anyway? It's miles away, across the sea,' she said. Johnny, however, couldn't stop thinking about what he'd been told ... a fortune was waiting for him in London, he *had* to go and find it.

Now Johnny and his wife had a little jar that they kept their savings in, but there wasn't an awful lot of money in there, for they never managed to do more than just scrape by. Johnny took half of their little store of cash and put it in his pocket, then he picked up his shovel, kissed his wife goodbye, and told her he was off to London to find his fortune. I won't tell you what his wife said, because you never know who might be listening to a story, but you can use your own imagination for that bit. Suffice it to say *she wasn't happy*. Off went Johnny down the path, and he turned to wave goodbye. He took one last look at his little white cottage, with the elder tree beside the door, the roof that sagged in the middle, the thorn tree at the base of the chimney and the big lump of stone in the garden that he'd never managed to shift out of the way. He blew his wife a final kiss ... from a safe distance ... and off he went.

Of course, not having much money, it took him ever such a long time to get to London. First of all, he had to get work on a ship, using his spade to shovel coal into the engine, so that he could cross the sea. When he landed in England his wages covered the cost of a train ticket ... but not one that took him all the way to London ... so he had to get another job, using his shovel to dig a canal, and the wages from *that job* got him to London ... eventually.

His shovel was pretty battered by now, and he'd been months on the journey, but off he went to London Bridge and he began to dig. Within a few minutes a man came up to him and asked him what he was doing. 'One of Themselves told me to come to London Bridge and dig, and I would get a fortune, so here I am.'

'That's funny,' said the other man. 'I'm from the Isle of Man myself, and I just had a dream that I was back there. I was in front of a little white cottage with a sagging roof and a thorn tree at the base of the chimney. There was an elder tree beside the door and a big lump of stone in the garden. In my dream I was told that if I would dig there, under the thorn tree, I would find a fortune. I'm not going to go though; the whole idea is foolish. I'm going to forget the whole thing and you should as well, for nobody will let you dig up London Bridge.'

He started to walk away, but Johnny called after him: 'Was there a woman in your dream?'

'Indeed there was,' the man replied. 'But she didn't look happy. I wouldn't want to get on the wrong side of her.' Johnny grinned and tried to carry on digging, but sure enough, people came to tell him to stop, or he'd be in trouble … so stop he did.

He thought about what the other man had said. It sounded like a description of *his* home and *his* wife, and if the only treasure he could get at was there, he'd better go back. Another four months it took him, to work his way back to the Island. He returned to his cottage in the dark, and he decided not to wake his wife until he had something of value to show her. There wasn't much blade left on his shovel by then, but he just about managed to dig under the thorn tree with it, and he found an iron box. He opened the box and it was full of gold!

In the morning he showed it to his wife, to prove he'd been right to listen to the little man's advice. All she said was, 'Why didn't the little man just tell you about the gold that was here, rather than sending you on a fool's errand to London? That's what I want to know.' She smiled at Johnny though, and he knew he was forgiven, for his wild goose chase had led him to a fortune in the end. His wife started to count the coins and found a piece of paper at the bottom of the iron box. Neither of them could read it, since it was in a foreign language, so Johnny put it put in the blacksmith's window, with a sign challenging anyone who could read it to tell them what it said. They offered a small reward, in the hope that someone would be able to explain it to them.

Eventually a young man came forward, who said it was in Latin and it meant 'Dig again and you'll find another'. Johnny bought himself a new shovel … well, he could afford to now … and he dug deeper under the thorn tree. Sure enough he dug up another iron box full of gold!

Johnny was delighted, and even his wife was pleased, so every night for the rest of his life, he would open the front door before he went to bed, and call out: 'My blessing on the Little Fellows.'

His wife, though she was grateful, never added her voice to his, because she still couldn't see why the little man played such a trick on them, making Johnny find the gold the hard way … by going all the way to London instead looking at home in the first place. Truth to tell, she had missed her man while he was away … not that she'd ever admit it, of course.

❧

This is from *Manx Fairy Tales* by Sophia Morrison (1911).

9

BEWARE OF
DANGEROUS ANIMALS

THE MODDEY DOO, OR THE BLACK DOG OF PEEL

Long ago, Peel Castle, on the west coast of the Island, always had a garrison of soldiers living in it. The ruins, which are very substantial, can still be visited, and as you walk in through the great gate there is a guardroom just inside, on the right. This was the room where the guards could relax if they were on duty but had no tasks to attend to for a while other than guarding the gate. It was in this room that the story takes place and long ago there was a dark underground passage that used to lead from this room and burrow under one of the old churches, coming out near to the captain of the guard's room. At the end of each day the soldiers would take it in turns to lock the castle gates and carry the keys through this passage to the captain. You could go round the outside of the buildings, above ground, but it was a longer journey … and a colder, wetter one too in winter.

One night they noticed that a strange black dog, a huge creature with long curly hair, had started to appear around the castle. Nobody knew anything about him … and nobody claimed to own him. It was as if he had materialised out of nowhere. The soldiers thought that there was something 'otherworldly' about him. He was never seen to eat or drink, never uttered a single bark or growl, and he only appeared at night, when he would walk out of the dark passageway into the room, his eyes glowing red in the firelight. The dog would then lie down next to the fire in the guardroom, just as the candles were being lit. He would usually stay there, still and silent, until morning, then stand up and return to the dark passageway. While the dog was there, the soldiers tried to be on their best behaviour, not singing or shouting or swearing, because the creature's presence made them nervous. The soldiers gradually lost their fear of him, especially when the men were all together in a group, but nobody wanted to be alone with the animal. The guards took to walking through the dark passageway in pairs when they carried the castle keys to the captain's room at the end of the day, for fear of meeting the Black Dog, or Moddey Doo, on their own.

Then one night a soldier, who had been on leave all day, came back drunk. He reached the gate, just as the others were about to lock it up, and snatched the keys off them as soon as they had been turned in the locks. The soldier had been drinking all day, and had reached that stage of drunkenness where he thought

he was invincible. He was convinced that he could do far more drunk than he could when he was sober, and do it better to boot! He was wrong, of course, because he was so drunk that he could barely stand up, but the drink had given him courage, and when he stumbled into the guardroom and saw the big Black Dog lying there, he started to boast, saying, 'I'm not afraid of the big Black Dog … I'm not afraid of anything, me, and to prove it I'm going to take these keys through the underground passage *on my own* and deliver them to the captain of the guard.' The other guards tried to dissuade him, reminding him that he wasn't on duty, he didn't need to deliver the keys, and if the captain saw him so drunk he'd get into trouble. The drunken soldier just shouted and swore, and when his friends reminded him again about the dog, the man went over and kicked the creature, to prove that he wasn't afraid, and dared the Black Dog to follow him. Still clutching the keys, the fellow set off into the darkness … and the Black Dog got up slowly from beside the fire, and followed him into the underground passage.

The other soldiers stared at each other in horror. They each felt that somebody should do something, but they were all frozen with fear. There was a dead silence in the guardhouse for a few minutes, then dreadful, unearthly screams and shouts were heard, coming from the passageway. The men were too terrified to move. Finally the drunken soldier stumbled back into the room. His face was pale and twisted with fear, his hair was standing on end, his mouth was moving … but he couldn't say a word. He died three days later, without ever being able to speak properly and tell his friends what had happened to him, and the Black Dog wasn't seen at the castle again.

But after that, nobody was willing to take that dark journey again, not in pairs, not in groups, not in whole battalions, so eventually the entrance to the passageway, where it came out into the guardroom, was bricked up, and the keys were always carried to the captain of the guard by taking the other, longer route. People said to the guards that now the passage was sealed off they could relax. But they didn't relax, did they? They just sat there, staring

at the place where the entrance to the passageway used to be ...
worrying ... in case the Black Dog came back *through the wall!*

This is one of the two best-known stories on the Island (the other
being 'The Buggane of St Trinian's') and it crops up in every collection of Manx fairy tales or Manx folklore.

The Cabbyl-Ushtey

The cabbyl-ushtey is another unusual Manx creature ... a water
horse. Now a water horse sounds like a lovely animal, doesn't it?
Well, it's not, as those of you who were paying attention earlier
know. It can be very, very dangerous!

The cabbyl-ushtey live in rivers, ponds and steams. They try
to attract people to follow them into the water and drown.
The people around Glen Maye believed that the glen below the
waterfall was haunted by the spirit of a man who met a cabbyl-
ushtey one day, and, thinking it was an ordinary horse, got up on
its back to ride it. At that moment the horse ran off and disappeared into the water, and the rider was drowned.

Once somebody wanders into the water, attracted by the cabbyl-
ushtey, the water horse then drags its victim below the surface and
rips them to shreds. However, it's not just people that are drawn
to the water horse, the cabbyl-ushtey attracts both humans and
livestock. It might seize cows and tear them to pieces, stampede
horses, or steal children ... nothing like a bit of variety.

Another tactic of the cabbyl-ushtey is to terrify a group of
people or a herd of cattle, causing its victims to scatter and run
away. This enables the cabbyl-ushtey to pick the slowest and
weakest person or animal to kill.

A farmer whose herd was dwindling went to investigate.
He knew some of his cows were disappearing, but he couldn't work
out who or what was taking them. Then he saw a cabbyl-ushtey

rise from the water of a nearby pond and rip one of his grazing cows into pieces. After he'd recovered from the shock, he wisely decided to protect the rest of his herd by moving them to another field, further away from the water. It took him the rest of the day to shift his herd to safety, but sadly, while he was doing this, his daughter, who he'd forgotten to warn, went down to the pond looking for a missing calf, and the cabbyl-ushtey took her.

When he got home that night, pleased with himself for saving the remainder of his herd, he found his wife clutching his daughter's bloodied shawl, which she'd found at the edge of the pond when she, in her turn, had gone looking for the girl. The farmer never forgave himself, for he had been so busy protecting his beloved cows that he never spared a thought for his greatest treasure … his daughter.

These stories are from *The Folklore of the Isle of Man* by A.W. Moore (1891).

The Pig of Plenty

The Arc-Vuc-Sonney, the Pig of Plenty, was an apparition that was sometimes seen to cross a man's path on a fine moonlit night, in the form of a young pig. If anyone spotted it, there was great excitement, because as long as a person could keep it in sight and follow it, it led him or her to great good luck. However, the moment the person took their eyes off the pig, it would vanish, and the good luck with it.

It was, of course, considered fortunate to see the Pig of Plenty, and if a fisherman saw it at the start of the fishing season, he was sure to be lucky. Even better than seeing the pig was catching it, for if anybody succeeded in doing that, their fortune was made. Naturally, catching a ghostly pig, in the dark, is not an easy task, so nobody knows for sure if anyone has ever succeeded.

There is another complication, too, which is that not *every* encounter with an unearthly pig is lucky.

There was once a boy who followed a fairy pig. The little creature was snow-white, with a feathery tail spread out like a fan, and long flapping ears that hung low enough to sweep the heather. When the animal turned to look at him, its eyes glowed like fire. It led the boy to the edge of a cliff, and would have had him plunge over it, but the child realised the danger just in time. The boy turned and ran towards his home but the pig chased after him all the way, until the boy reached his cottage and safety. His grandmother was convinced that this had been a fairy pig, and she was worried. She had good reason to be, because soon after the encounter the child sickened, and became so ill that his family were alarmed.

The lad couldn't eat or sleep, he was running a fever, and had a terrible stabbing pain in his right leg. His health got worse and worse until at last his parents had him carried to a charmer in Castletown. If he had had a mortal illness, they would have taken him to a doctor, but since they were sure his sickness was of fairy origin, a charmer was definitely the person to see.

Now a male charmer was called a fer-obbee, and a female charmer was a ben-obbee, and both would use certain formulas and ceremonies to cure diseases. They could use their powers to counteract the spells of fairies and of witches, as well as supplying medicinal herbs to treat various conditions. These powers were said to be handed down in the same family for generations, and people had great faith in the charmers' abilities.

The charmer the boy was taken to was male, a fer-obbee, and he looked at the painful leg and said that the boy's calf had been punctured with fairy shot, then he got out an old book and opened it at a picture of a little plant. The charmer pointed to the picture with his left hand, while he used his right hand to make the sign of the cross on the boy's right leg, and said, 'I spread this fairy shot in the name of the Father, and of the Son, and of the Holy Ghost. If it is a fairy shot, in the name of the Lord, I spread it out of the flesh, out of the sinews, and out of the bones.'

At that moment the pain stopped and the boy returned to health, though the charmer warned his parents that the lad was not to go out on to the mountain alone in the dark again. The boy stayed healthy after that, and all he had to show for his adventure was a mark on his leg where the stab went through, as clear as glass to the bone.

So there's the problem, you see ... if you spot a pig on a moonlit night, when you're on your own, what should you do? Chase after it, in case it's the Pig of Plenty bringing you good fortune, or avoid it, in case it's a fairy pig that's trying to kill you? I'll leave it to you to decide.

ॐ

The Pig of Plenty appears in *William Cashen's Manx Folklore* by William Cashen (1912), and the tale of the boy and the fairy pig is from *Manx Fairy Tales* by Sophia Morrison (1911).

Information about the charmers appears in *The Folklore of the Isle of Man* by A.W. Moore (1891) and in *What to do if your Dad's been exchanged for a Fairy* by Andrea Byrne (2003).

The Tarroo-Ushtey

Remember the tale of the cabbyl-ushtey, the water horse? Well this is the story of the tarroo-ushtey, the water bull. If you were to see this creature in a field by daylight, you'd never be able to tell that it wasn't a normal bull ... but then, something odd would happen. The next time you went out to check on your cows, half of your herd would have vanished ... and so would the bull!

This is because the tarroo-ushtey will trot up and join a herd of cows out in a field, and for a while, he'll do what bovines do. He'll graze for a bit, and then nuzzle up to one or two of them and generally get himself accepted. This seems to be straightforward, as cows are foolishly trusting creatures. Sometime later, he'll look up and stare fixedly in one direction, as if he's spotted something enticing. Then he'll gallop off towards this invisible delight, with half the herd following behind him, thinking that he must know of some delicious treat that they were unaware of.

ॐ

In fact, what he knows of is a deep pool, or a river, which he'll dive into, the cows following close behind. Being an amphibious creature, this is easy enough for the tarroo-ushtey, but it's not so easy for the cows, which, not being amphibious themselves, all drown. That seems to be the point, for him to lead the cows away and drown them. What he does with them after that is rather more difficult to investigate. Perhaps he eats them, perhaps he just destroys them to spite the farmer, it's hard to be quite sure.

Stories of tarroo-ushtey used to abound on the Island. Long ago there was a farmer who kept cattle, and his fields became infested by such a creature. Several cows had been lost to the water bull already, and the farmer was determined not to lose any more. He had a number of men working for him, so he got them to take it in turn to keep watch over the herd, and warn him if a strange bull appeared. He had good reason to be concerned because, as well as leading the cows into deep water to drown them, it was believed that if the creature mated with one of the cows the resulting calf would be a misshapen lump of flesh and skin, without any bones, and the cow itself would die giving birth to it.

Well, the men kept their watch, and sure enough, in the middle of the night, a strange bull appeared. In the darkness the tarroo-ushtey's eyes were large, and sparkled like fire. There was no doubt that this was a magical and malevolent creature. The farmer quickly organised his men, who grabbed poles and pitchforks and began to chase the water bull. The animal was too clever for them, however, and having led them up hill and down dale until the men were exhausted, he dived into a river, too deep for the men to wade in after him. There swam the water bull, bobbing his head up and down, staring at them, as if he was mocking them, which perhaps he was.

This account comes from *The Folklore of the Isle of Man* by A.W. Moore (1891).

THE DEVIL'S DEN

Now I don't know about you, but I've got a bit of a soft spot for dragons … from a safe distance anyway. Now there are all sorts of strange creatures on the Island, but dragons aren't among them, or so I thought, until I came across this old tale.

They say that up near Barrule, where the wizard Manannan used to live, there is a hole in the ground, just at the foot of the mountain, which they call 'The Devil's Den'. This place, perhaps because of being so close to the seat of Manannan's power, seems to have special, magical properties.

Long ago, in the days of enchantment, the magicians who came after Manannan was banished, used the cave to imprison anyone, or anything, they wished to contain. The kind of creatures, and people, that could not be held captive in an ordinary prison. The kind that the wizards, for whatever reason, hoped would never see the light of day again.

Of course, where there's a hole in the ground, there are people who want to climb in and explore it. These days such people are spelunkers, or speleologists, bat workers doing hibernation surveys, or just plain cavers, but in the past they were generally called 'reckless idiots' ... or names to that effect. Some of these 'reckless ...' sorry ... these cavers ... were determined to find out what was in The Devil's Den, but it turned out to be harder to enter the cave than people expected.

You see, some people would try to ride their horses up to the cave, but as soon as the horse neared the entrance its hair would stand on end, and its eyes would stare, and a damp sweat would cover its whole body. The same went for dogs that were taken up there, and any other animals placed in the vicinity of the cave. Now you might be thinking that none of that matters ... that you don't need a horse, or a dog, or someone's pet gerbil to explore a hole in the ground. But if you've just seen animals behaving like that and then you hear strange noises coming out of the dark pit, well, you might start to feel a little differently about climbing down there.

And then there were the stories ... according to one, the cave contains a great and powerful prince – so powerful that the wizards wanted him out of the way. This prince has been bound there by magic spells for well over seven hundred years, without ever knowing death or daylight. Though what state he's in now we may never know ... is he even in human form? And would you want to be the person to find out?

You see there *is* an eyewitness account (by the great-grandfather of somebody now long dead, but an eyewitness account none the less) that he saw a dragon. A huge dragon, with a tail and wings that darkened the whole sky as it flew over his head. Its eyes seemed to be two globes of fire, which helped it to see as it descended swiftly into The Devil's Den, and after it had vanished underground, the man heard the most terrible shrieks and groans coming from within the cave. Perhaps the captive prince has been transformed into a dragon … or perhaps both prince and dragon co-exist in the darkness. Perhaps we'll never know, because nobody is brave enough to go and look!

Found in *The Folklore of the Isle of Man* by A.W. Moore (1891).

THE MAGIC MONGOOSE

The Isle of Man has been home to many strange creatures over the years, and in recent times one of the strangest was Geoff, the Dalby Spook, who became well known in the 1930s. Geoff was a talking mongoose, who hid himself behind the panelling in an old farmhouse in Dalby, on the west side of the Island.

It was Mary who heard him first, back in 1931. She was nine, the youngest in the family, and a happy, pretty little thing. She noticed a tapping sound behind the panelling in the sitting room. Old houses can be full of strange creaking and groaning sounds, so she wasn't particularly concerned about it. Then she saw something scurrying across the floor. At first she thought it might be a ra … a long-tail. Then she realised that the body was too long, and the tail was hairy, not bald. There was something odd about its legs too, but she couldn't get a good enough look at it.

She told other members of the family, and at first they thought she'd imagined it, but after a while they began to catch glimpses of it too. Out came the encyclopaedia and different animals were looked up, to try and identify the unusual creature. They came to the conclusion that it was a sort of mongoose, although it did seem to have fingers instead of claws. That wasn't the strangest thing about it though, because soon they all heard it whispering behind the walls in a human voice … sometimes in English or Manx, sometimes in foreign languages. Geoff, as they called it, was very fond of Mary, and he always talked more when she was around.

When word got out, various visitors came to try and see or hear the Dalby Spook. Over the next four years the family was visited by everyone from ghost hunters to cryptozoologists, and journalists, of course, lots of journalists, but although they sometimes heard him, Geoff always hid from strangers. Language experts would listen, with their ears against the walls, and announce that Geoff was speaking Italian … or French … or Spanish, but hearing him was all they ever achieved. Once the visitors had gone, however, Geoff would reappear and he would even mimic the visitors' voices, which the family found very entertaining.

He never caused any harm to anyone, though if he was annoyed he would break dishes, and throw things round the room. Most of the time he seemed fairly content, and the happier he was the more they would hear him tapping or chattering behind the panelling.

Perhaps the most unusual characteristic of this remarkable creature was that he could predict the future a little, telling members of the family details of events that were about to happen, or announcing who would be arriving at the farmhouse over the next few days.

Almost always, Geoff was right. Some people speculated that he was a poltergeist or ghost, while others were convinced that it was a real animal … a freak of nature. The family stopped worrying about what he was – it's amazing what you can get used to – and to them he was just Geoff.

Sometime in 1935 the house went quiet and Geoff was seen no more. They never knew what had happened, whether he was a real animal that died, or a strange spirit that had moved on. All the family knew was that they missed him, Mary most of all. Bizarre as the creature was, she had grown to love him, and she mourned his loss just as any of us would grieve over the death of a beloved pet.

The Dalby Spook is mentioned in *Fables, Fantasies and Folklore of the Isle of Man* by Harry Penrice (1996).

10

Manx Customs and Traditional Beliefs

Goggins

On Twelfth Night, 6 January, which is the last day of Christmas, teenage girls on the Island would sometimes play a type of game, to predict what sort of man they would marry. It was done in fun … just like we used to say 'Tinker, tailor, soldier, sailor, rich man, poor man, beggar man, thief' when counting the fruit stones in our puddings – the last stone counted was supposed to predict the profession of one's future husband.

Well, on the Isle of Man, the girls would gather up some little things that might represent what job their future husband would do – these items were called goggins – and they would put these bits and pieces into wooden cups in front of the fireplace. Then each girl would be sent out of the room in turn, while the others would swap all the cups around. The girl would come back into the room blindfolded, and choose a wooden cup. The goggins in it were supposed to represent the job that the girl's future husband would do … the type of man she would marry.

If a girl picked a cup with water in, it meant she would marry a sailor.

A tiny piece of lead meant a miner.

A little piece of wood represented a carpenter.

A cross meant she'd marry a vicar.

Some grains of corn stood for a farmer.

And cloth meant the girl who picked it would marry a tailor.

But once, when a group of girls were playing the game, something rather unpredictable happened. One poor girl was very unlucky … she came into the room blindfolded and picked her cup, but when she put her hand in it to pull out the goggins, she pulled out a dead rat! (Sorry … long-tail. Traditionally nobody ever uses the R.A.T. word on the Island, the term long-tail is always substituted!)

So … she put her hand into the cup and pulled out … a dead long-tail!

Everyone wondered how it got in there, but nobody knew for sure … it must have been sick, and crawled in there to die. Well, all the other girls teased her and laughed at her … you can imagine the sort of thing they said: 'She's going to marry a dead long-tail, she's going to marry a dead long-tail, she's going to marry a dead long-tail ...'

Well, time passed, and off the others went and married the men the goggins had predicted, farmers and sailors, miners and tailors ... one of them married a carpenter, and one even married a vicar ... but the girl who got the dead long-tail had the last laugh, for eventually she met and married ... can anyone guess? ... *An undertaker ... a man who dealt with the dead.* And a rich undertaker at that ... so the goggins were right after all.

⬎

The term 'goggins' can also refer to the cups used in the game. I came across this story in *More Manx Myths* by Dennis W. Turner (2005) and it is such fun ... so long as you don't say the R.A.T. word when telling it on the Island, or the whole audience will be knocking on wood repeatedly to counteract the bad luck! It can get very noisy!

THE OLD CHRISTMAS

We all know what day Christmas falls on, don't we? On 25 December! Every year! Despite the fact that the date *always* creeps up on those people who leave their Christmas shopping until the last minute. We tend to forget that the calendar has changed ... I mean the calendar of the years and the seasons. Nowadays we celebrate Christmas on 25 December, but long ago 6 January was believed to be the true Christmas Day, and many people continued to believe that that *was* the real Christmas Day, even hundreds of years after the calendar was changed. This was true on the Island as well, where memories are long, and traditions die hard.

Now once 25 December was considered to be Christmas Day, the tradition built up that on the first day of the Christmas

holidays the spinning wheels all had to be put away, the making
of nets ceased, and no work of any kind was to be done until after
Twelfth Day, 6 January, which was now the last day of Yule.

But there was once an old woman called Peggy who was determined to finish some spinning that she had started just before
Christmas. All through the festivities, the knowledge of this
unfinished piece of work nibbled away at her. It wasn't just that
she wanted to get it done, but she knew how fast she could knit
clothing from the finished yarn, and what she could charge for
the clothes that she knitted, since everyone knew how good her
work was.

Peggy liked money, and she liked working, and the long winter
holidays, when everyone was meant to relax and enjoy themselves,
were an agony to her. So on Old Christmas Eve, 5 January, she said
to herself, 'The New Christmas is past and surely it can't do any
harm to do a bit of spinning tonight, the holiday is almost over.'
She wasn't completely sure about that, but she was determined to
finish the task. So when her husband and the rest of the family
were in bed, she called her young servant girl, Margad, and said,
'The two of us will finish the spinning tonight, Margad.'

Margad was frightened that they would get into trouble
somehow, but she got out her wheel, as she had been told, and sat
beside her mistress. The two began to spin, and they were spinning
and spinning until almost midnight. The young girl grew weary
with working, but her mistress insisted that they both carry on.
Then just before midnight old Peggy saw the flax she was drawing
from the distaff grow blacker and blacker till it was as black as tar.
It was ruined, and could never be knitted into anything ... but
Margad's flax did not change colour because she had only done
what her mistress bade her. Peggy dropped her flax quickly, put
away her wheel, and crept to bed in fear. She knew now which
was the true Christmas Day and never more did she spin on Old
Christmas Eve.

Margad was left alone in the kitchen after her mistress had gone,
clearing up the rest of the flax. At first she trembled with fright,
but she was a brave girl, and she had an idea. Usually she would

have been sent to her bed by this time, but since, just this once, there was no one to tell her what she could and couldn't do, she decided to go outside, to see if all the things that she had heard about Old Christmas Eve were true.

She had heard that the bees came out, and the bullocks knelt and the myrrh came into bloom, and she wanted to see these wonders for herself.

So she put on a cloak and crept out of the door into the cold frosty moonlit night, just as midnight struck. She stooped to look at the spot where the myrrh root was buried, for it was the custom to grow Sweet Cicely in Manx gardens. This aromatic plant was called 'Myrrh', and Margad loved it because it tasted and smelt of aniseed. As the girl crouched over to look at the myrrh root, the earth began to stir and to crack, and soon two little green shoots pushed up to the air. She bent closer to see what would happen, and to her great wonder the leaves and stalks grew big and strong before her eyes, and then the buds began to show, and in a few minutes the lovely white flowers were in bloom and the garden was sweet with their scent. Margad could do nothing but stare at them at first, but at last she dared to gather one small piece of the blossom, and she kept it for luck all her life.

Then she went to the cowshed and peeped through the door. She heard a groaning sound and there were the young bullocks on their knees, moaning, and the sweat was dropping from them. Margad knelt down, too, in the cowshed, and said a bit of a prayer to the Holy Child that was born in a stable. But the wonders were not over yet, for as she went silently back to the house she noticed that the bees were out and they were singing and flying around their hive. By the time the girl shut the door of the house behind her, the bees had gone back into the hive, and the magical hour was over.

Always after that, when people asked her if she believed in the wonders of the Old Christmas Eve, she would reply, 'I know that it's true, for I've seen it for myself.'

⁂

This can be found in *Manx Fairy Tales* by Sophia Morrison (1911) and another version of it is in *The Green Glass Bottle – Folk Tales from the Isle of Man* by Zena Carus (1975).

GOOSEFLOWERS

Daffodils are such bright and cheerful flowers, always seen as a sign of spring, and they grow abundantly, so it's natural to see bunches of them in vases on tables and on windowsills … except on the Island, where bringing daffodils into the house was thought to be unlucky. You might wonder where such a superstition came from … and believe it or not, it came from geese, or rather, the importance of geese.

You see, not everyone on the Island could afford to have cows or sheep, but most people could have a few geese. They could be grazed on common land and after harvest they could be fed on stubble. Then they were killed, cut into four quarters and salted down in barrels. Even a single quarter could make a good-sized pot of broth or stew for a family, so they were an important supply of meat for families who couldn't afford such a luxury often.

Now there would usually be a fire in the hearth, with a cupboard beside it, and in the past the goose was often put in there, in the warmth, to hatch her eggs, and there the goose would sit, with the cupboard door open, of course, diligently sitting on her clutch of eggs. Sometimes children would come in with bunches of daffodils for their mothers, but children being children, flowers would be dropped on the floor, as well as shoved into jugs or jars … and that's where the superstition came from.

Apparently the goose would see these bright yellow blooms on the floor, similar in size and colour to a gosling, and think that their brood had hatched. They would grow restless, stop incubating their eggs or even break them, so the children were told not to bring the bright yellow flowers into the house. Indeed, daffodils became nicknamed 'Gooseflowers', and were always blamed if goose eggs failed to hatch. I have to admit it does make me wonder about what kind of eyesight a goose must have to mistake a daffodil for a gosling … but I suppose it *is* easier to forbid people to bring daffodils into the house, than to fit a goose with glasses!

 ❧

Mentioned in *Legends of a Lifetime* by George E. Quayle (1973), and *More Manx Myths* by Dennis. W. Turner (2005).

THE BUMBY CAGE

Now I don't know what kind of punishments any younger ones among you get for being naughty, but I bet it doesn't involve being turned into something else, something 'not human'. But if you were a fairy, and you lived on the Isle of Man long ago, things were a little different.

Mothers on the Island used to tell their children that any fairies (or Little People, as they were called there) who had been naughty were punished by being turned into bumblebees. It was hoped that being a bumblebee for a while would teach them a lesson, and once they turned back into fairies, they would behave better in future!

Of course, lots of little children felt sorry for these naughty fairies, and wanted to help them learn their lesson and change back into their fairy form as quickly as possible. So to help them help the fairies, the children's mothers would make a bumby cage! They were made of plaited rushes, woven basket-fashion like a baby's rattle. One end would be the handle, tightly plaited, the other would be wider, with room to tuck something inside it.

The children would take this cage out into the meadows and hunt for a bee tucked into a flower, collecting pollen. They'd place the cage over the end of the flower, so when the bee flew out it would be trapped in a little bumby prison cell, and the children would twist the rushes at the wide end, to keep the creature inside. The idea was that this extra temporary punishment would help the magical little creature learn to be good even more quickly – breaking the spell so that they could turn back into a fairy almost immediately.

Once the children were asleep in bed their mothers would undo the top of the bumby cage and set the bee free, then close up the cage again. When the children woke up and saw that the cage was empty, they were sure the bee had changed back into a fairy and flown away, to join the others of their kind. As for the bumblebees themselves, they were probably just pleased to be free!

❧

This pastime is mentioned in *Legends of a lifetime* by George E. Quayle (1973) and in *Manx Myths and More* by Dennis W. Turner (2003).

This sounds like a much more recent approach to fairies than is found in most Manx tales. The fairies would have to be pretty small to turn into bees and be caged in a bumby. The idea of them flying off is also not typically Manx. The Little People on the Island are traditionally about three foot tall, and they don't fly, though they do love to ride horses. However, as an Island tradition, it is great fun, and deserves a place in this collection.

MANX BLESSING, OR A CHARM TO WARD OFF FAIRIES

Shee Yee as shee ghooinney,
Shee Yee er Columb-Killey
Er dagh uinnag, er dagh dorrys.
Er dagh towl goaill stiagh yn Re-hollys.
Er kiare corneillyn y thie
Er y voayl ta mee my lhie
As shee Yee orrym-pene.

Peace of God and peace of man,
Peace of God on Columb-Killey.

❧

On each window and each door,
On every hole admitting moonlight,
On the four corners for the house,
On the place of my rest,
And the peace of God on myself!

∾

This is from *Manx Fairy Tales* by Sophia Morrison (1911) and other sources.

Columb-Killey is the Manx for St Columba. 'Laa Columb-Killey' means St Columba's Day (or literally) the Day of the church of St Columba. In ancient times the festival was held on the anniversary of the day on which St Columba died on the steps of the altar in the cathedral of Iona, which was Whit Sunday, 597. It was customary that the service in the church (Arbory church being dedicated to St Columba) should be followed by public games and rejoicings, and when the people were gathered together there was a tendency to start doing a bit of trading in the churchyard.

This is supposed to be the origin of the Manx fairs. Eventually it was forbidden to hold gatherings in the churchyards and they were moved to the village 'green' or common land. After 1752, when the New Calendar Act came into operation, the old style was observed in keeping the fairs in the Island, and Columba's Fair – styled 'Ballabeg Fair' in later years – was therefore held on 22 June. Recently, the festival has been revived, and is now always held on the Thursday nearest the above date.

THE WHITE LADY

Now most of the stories in this collection are old, very old. This one, however, is a little bit old and a little bit new. Starting with the old, there are some very big rocks on the Island, and the stone in this tale, The White Lady, is one of them. Some of them are set in stone circles, some mark graves, historical and prehistoric, and some, like this one, mark the site of a keeill, an early Christian chapel, and a cemetery. Bronze Age cremations were found near this stone in the past and several coffins were uncovered.

These traces are now long gone, but the stone is still there. Now that may not sound remarkable to you, as I said there are stones all over the Island ... but those are all in desolate places, the kind of places where people are happy to leave well alone. This stone, well, this stone is a little bit different, because of where it is.

It is known as The White Lady of First Avenue, which makes it sound like a cross between an ancient ghost and an American President's wife. I have to say it's not that glamorous to look at, but it is impressive none the less. It's a bulbous standing stone of white quartz, wider at the base than the top, and taller than a person ... well, than this person anyway. It glints rather nicely in the sunlight, but the most exceptional thing about it is that it's in the middle of Douglas, the capital city of the Isle of Man, and it's in the middle of the road! Not in a pretty, decorative, centre of a roundabout kind of way, but in a 'taking up one half of the road and cars can jolly well edge round it' kind of way.

There are kerbstones encircling it, from the edge of the pavement, around the rock (giving it a wide birth) and back to the pavement again. This protuberance narrows the road, which has to curve around it, whereas it is much more usual for roads to go where planners and architects decide they should go, and anything that gets in the way is generally shifted or flattened.

So what is The White Lady still doing there? Well, that brings us to the newer part of this story, which occurred in the 1930s. The decision was made back then that Douglas needed a new residential area, and First Avenue was going to be the start of it. Central to the town and not far from Government House, it was the perfect location. The roads and houses were all planned, and nobody seemed that bothered that The White Lady was still there, partially blocking one of the proposed roads.

According to the legend, the builder told his men to move the stone, so that the road could run as planned, but somehow the men kept putting it off. Some people said the stone made eerie noises when the workforce tried to move it; others claimed that it was the rumours that started flying that alarmed the men.

People began to mention a curse that would befall anyone who moved the stone, that disaster would strike the one who caused it to fall, and any who were foolish enough to help him. The builder heard these whispers too, and at first he tried to dismiss them, but the people of the Isle of Man don't take their legends lightly. The builder could have forced or bullied his men into shifting the stone regardless, or even done the job himself, and yet ... he couldn't bring himself to do it. Instead, he realigned the road to bend around the stone and The White Lady won that encounter. She's still standing there, smugly taking up half the road, to this day. I know, because I've seen her, and you can too, if you're ever in Douglas!

◦

I came across this story in *More Manx Myths* by Dennis. W. Turner (2005) and I came across The White Lady on First Avenue, in Douglas!

Some people put the whole incident down to sympathetic town planning; in which case, let's have more of it. But me, I choose to believe the story ... only on the Isle of Man can a legend win against planners and builders. You know what they say, 'The best laid plans of mice and men often go awry' ... and this time, it seems, they did!

MANX TARTAN

There was once a weaver called Samuel, who lived in Laxey. He wanted to weave a piece of cloth that represented the Isle of Man and all the best things on it, but he couldn't decide what colour of thread to use, so Samuel asked everyone he knew what colour *they* thought the cloth should be.

He went to his best friend, who was a fisherman, and asked him what colour to use, and his friend said that the cloth must be blue, the colour of the sea surrounding the Island.

He asked his neighbour, the shepherd, who said the cloth should be green, like the hills.

He asked the children, and they told him it should be gold, like the gorse, the colour of sunshine.

He asked his mother, who told him it should be purple, like the heather, for heather was lucky and would remind them all how fortunate they were to live on the Island, and share it with all the magical creatures there.

He asked his wife, who loved their little home, and she said that he should use white to represent all the cottages on the Island.

Now Samuel was completely confused. He couldn't use all those colours, could he? If he wove them all in randomly, the cloth would just look a mess, so he went out for a walk to clear his head. He climbed up a hill and looked around. He could see all the colours that his friends and his family had suggested he use in the landscape around him, but how could he weave them all into one cloth? And anyway it left out the farmers … all the little fields he could see, spread out before him, they ought to be woven into the cloth too. He looked again … *all the little fields* … they would be his pattern. He would weave a tartan, a Manx tartan, and the criss-cross of the different coloured threads would form the fields!

So Samuel went home to Laxey and wove the first Manx Tartan … and it went like this:

Blue for the Sea,
Green for the Hills,
Gold for the Gorse,
Purple for the Heather
And White for the Cottages!

All forming a pattern of little squares, just like the farmers' fields.

And so the Manx Tartan has stayed to this day, just as the weaver designed it all those years ago!

And just as the colours of the Manx Tartan represent all that is best about the Island, I hope that these stories do too!

❧

This verse is from the Laxey Woollen Mills, where the Manx Tartan is woven, and the mill's Managing Director, John Wood, has kindly given me permission to use it, both in my storytellings, and in print.

Pronunciations

Arc-Vuc-Sonney	*Arc-Vuck-Sonna*
Ben-obbee	*Ben-obi*
Ben-varrey	*Ben-varra*
Buggane	*Bugair-n*
Cabbyl-ushtey	*Cavyl-ushcha* (ushtey means water in Manx)
Columb-Killey	*Colum-Killya*
Dooinney marrey	*Dunnya marra*
Dooiney-oie	*Dunya-ee*
Fer-obbee	*Fur-obi*
Glashtin	*Glash-chen*
Keimagh	*K-mackh*
Lag ny Keeilley	*Lag na Killya*
Lhiannan shee	*Lyannan she*
Lugh dhoan	*Luch dawn*
Manannan Mac Y Leirr	*Manannan Mac Lear*
Margad	*Margud*
Moddey Doo	*Mawtha Do*
Mollychreest	*Mollerchreest*
Mollyndroat	*Mollndroat*
Mooinjer-Veggey	*Munjar-Vega*
Phynodderee	*Phen-or-deree*
Purr Mooar	*Poor Moo-er*
Scaa goanlyssagh	*Scare gorn-lissachk*
Shoh Slaynt	*Sho Slant*
Slieu Whallian	*Slew Whallian*
St Maughold	*St Mac-cold*
Tarroo-ushtey	*Tarroo-ushcha*
Traa-dy-liooar	*Trair-de-lure*

ABOUT THE
AUTHOR

FIONA ANGWIN performs across the country as a storyteller and puppeteer, working as The Yarn Spinner (www.theyarnspinner.com), and is a member of the Society for Storytelling. She is also a freelance actress and writer, her novel *Soul-Lights* is available from Priory Press Ltd on the Isle of Man, and other outlets, and the sequel is soon to follow. She builds puppets, for her own work and for other people, as Touchstone Puppets (www.touchstonepuppets.com).

In addition she is a zoologist and licensed bat worker, and has used this in conjunction with her theatre training to create conservation-based theatre projects, as well as working as an artistic director, drama teacher, theatre administrator, workshop leader, bat officer, veterinary assistant and zookeeper/presenter at Chester Zoo. Fiona is currently involved in creating touring productions with Off Book Theatre, alongside her storytelling work.

Her enjoyment in creating this book reflects her interest in and affection for the Isle of Man, its people, its history and its folk tales.

ABOUT THE ILLUSTRATOR

DENISE McCOID gained her Degree in Illustration in 2013. The illustrations in this book are her first commission for a book publication and she has been honoured to participate in such an exciting project. For more information on her work see:

www.facebook.com/MyArtandIllustrations

BIBLIOGRAPHY

Byrne, Andrea, *What to do if your Dad's been exchanged for a Fairy* (2003)

Callow, Edward, *The Phynodderee and Other Legends of the Isle of Man* (1882)

Carus, Zena, *The Green Glass Bottle – Folk Tales from The Isle of Man* (1975)

Cashen, William, *William Cashen's Manx Folklore* (1912)

Ifans, Rhiannon, *Tales from the Celtic Countries* (1999)

Kelly, Robert, *Tales of the Tailless* (2001)

Killip, Margaret, *The Folklore of the Isle of Man* (1975)

Moore, A.W., *The Folklore of the Isle of Man* (1891)

Morrison, Sophia, *Manx Fairy Tales* (1911)

Penrice, Henry, *Fables, Fantasies and Folklore of the Isle of Man* (1996)

Quayle, George E., *Legends of a Lifetime* (1979)

Reader's Digest Association, *The Most Amazing Places of Folklore & Legend in Britain* (2011)

Turner, Dennis W., *Manx Myths and More* (2003)

Turner, Dennis W., *More Manx Myths* (2005)

Also from The History Press

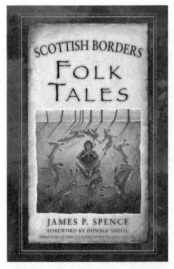

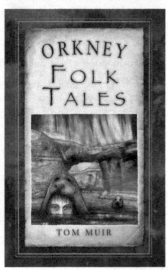

Find this title and more at
www.thehistorypress.co.uk

Also from The History Press

ΛNCIENT
LEGENDS
RETOLD

This series features some of the country's best-known folklore heroes. Each story is retold by master storytellers, who live and breathe these legends. From the forests of Sherwood to the Round Table, this series celebrates our rich heritage.

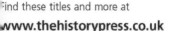

Society *for* **Storytelling**

Since 1993, the Society for Storytelling has championed the art of oral storytelling and the benefits it can provide – such as improving memory more than rote learning, promoting healing by stimulating the release of neuropeptides, or simply great entertainment! Storytellers, enthusiasts and academics support and are supported by this registered charity to ensure the art is nurtured and developed throughout the UK.

Many activities of the Society are available to all, such as locating storytellers on the Society website, taking part in our annual National Storytelling Week at the start of every February, purchasing our quarterly magazine *Storylines*, or attending our Annual Gathering – a chance to revel in engaging performances, inspiring workshops, and the company of like-minded people.

You can also become a member of the Society to support the work we do. In return, you receive free access to *Storylines*, discounted tickets to the Annual Gathering and other storytelling events, the opportunity to join our mentorship scheme for new storytellers, and more. Among our great deals for members is a 30% discount off titles in the *Folk Tales* series from The History Press website.

For more information, including how to join, please visit

www.sfs.org.uk